Also by Gregory Galloway

Just Thieves

As Simple As Snow

The 39 Deaths of Adam Strand

For Gina

and

ALL WE TRUST

I saved the house. I saw the smoke from the road and was there before the fire got out of control. Now he thinks I'm the one who started it. I didn't start it, but I'll finish it. Twenty years I've known the man, from the time he moved to town when we were still in high school through three wives—two for him and one for me—and working together on this and that (which was the cause of it all to begin with) and I never once envied what he had—never eyed his wives, never coveted his take, never wished I was in his place and had what he had—and now he accuses me, suspects me, and outright confronts me. He wants me to keep my mouth shut about it, but it's too late for that. It needs to be dragged out into the light.

If he wants a war, I'll give him a war. If he wants to play games, I'll play. But I'll play to win. I don't care if he's my neighbor, my business partner, whatever; if he comes after me, I'm going to come right back at him. I won't make the first move, but I will make the last. He can say what he wants, do what he wants, think what he wants, but I know what happened. The truth is on my side. We'll see if that counts for anything.

Let's take a good look at the facts and see who's to blame and who's in the right.

Al lives up the hill, about a mile and a half away on the same road. He has a good view of the valley, the river that runs below, and the road that always took us somewhere more interesting and always brought us back home. You can see the river from Al's, hugging the road as it curls toward town a few miles away. By the time it reaches the city, no one notices, as it flows underneath the streets for the most part, before winding away again. Al and I spent a lot of time sitting in his backyard and looking at the river. That's about all the attention it got from us; we rarely went into it, to fish or canoe or kayak. It's too shallow and rocky to put a boat into it, and Al and I were never much on fishing. So we'd just sit and drink beer and look down on it from his backyard and then forget all about it. It's a nice view from up the top of the hill, a better view than what I have, meadows and woods, but I can't complain. I see Al's view every day.

I take my dog Zeno for a walk by his place every morning. Al is never up that early and we rarely see him. We walked by just for the view, sometimes see the sun come up from the top of the hill, and once in a while it would be spectacular reds and oranges and pinks soaking the sky, spreading out for a moment and staining everything before dissipating as the sun moved. Zeno and I would admire it and then turn around and go home and have breakfast. We've done this every day since I got Zeno three years ago, a few days after my wife left me. Zeno and I have few complaints; the wife complained all the time. And she didn't want to go on walks.

The black smoke hung in the trees, like a noxious kite tail waiting to be untangled and set free. It was like a long arm reaching down the hill and pulling Zeno and me right to Al's house. I thought maybe Al was having trouble with his furnace, burning some bad oil or something, but then we saw the flames coming out of his garage. I called 911, then

Zeno and I went and looked and saw the fire in the corner. I tied Zeno to a tree and went around to the side door of the garage, thinking I'd break the window and get in that way, but the door was already open, the window already broken. I'd been in the garage so many times over the years I knew it as well as I knew my own house. Al had built a small office in it, a glass enclosure that had a desk, a sink, a small woodstove, and a refrigerator he kept stocked with beer. When he was married, we'd sit out by the woodstove and drink beer and talk, thinking of ways to make money without working. It was basically the same when he wasn't married, except we'd go to the house.

I opened the door and grabbed the fire extinguisher and had most of it out before the fire company arrived. They had to make a big production of things anyway, swinging axes and throwing around more water than required. They made a mess of it while Zeno and I stood in the yard and waited for them to leave. Al was nowhere to be found.

It turns out I won't be dead until tomorrow. Al called and said he was coming over to kill me, then called back about an hour later and said he had better things to do. "I'll get you tomorrow, though, you son of a bitch."

I don't think he's sworn at me the entire time I've known him. You can count the times we've argued on one hand, and over minor things, meaningless details of jobs or how to do things. I remember he got mad at me one time when I brought some warm beer over and he couldn't wait for it to get cooled down. "Who brings warm beer?" he said.

"I grabbed it from the cooler," I tried to tell him. "They must have just put it in. I didn't even check. I'll go back and get some cold."

"No," he said, as if it was some problem impossible to correct. "Who buys warm beer?" he muttered as he paced around the garage. Finally he found a fire extinguisher and brought it over. "Put the beer in that bucket," he said, nodding toward an empty bucket. I did as I was told and he pulled the pin on the extinguisher and blasted it at the beer.

"That's probably enough," I said after a good ten seconds or so, not knowing how long you actually needed to spray warm beer with a fire extinguisher to cool it down. I was more worried about the amount of crap I'd be putting my mouth around with all the stuff that was flying around the room.

Al kept firing. Finally, after maybe almost a minute, he stopped and went over to the bucket. He pulled out a beer and opened the can. The beer was mostly frozen.

"How about that," he said. "Anyway, I've got some beer in the house," he said and laughed.

"I'll get your fire extinguisher recharged," I said and put it in my car. That's the fire extinguisher I used in the garage. I knew exactly where it was because it hadn't moved from the spot where I put it the first time.

That was the worst fight we ever had, I think, until now. Now he's got this in his mind. Betrayal, I guess it is. Or maybe it's decades worth of unaired arguments, unresolved grievances and slights, big and small, bottled-up anger and resentment finally uncorked. Maybe he'll come to his senses. Once it all gets released, vented out like excess steam, he'll realize how silly the notion is. I wouldn't set his house on fire, and I wouldn't steal from him or cheat him or whatever else he thinks; I wouldn't do anything against him. I never have and I never will. We've been through too much. He'll realize that soon enough. Then again, maybe he'll kill me before that.

My daughter came home in time for dinner. Sara. Sixteen and driving and seems to only come home to eat and sleep. She came through the back door that led into the kitchen and I made her a plate and set it down in her spot. She sat down and took one look at me and said, "What's wrong with you?"

"Nothing," I said. "Al's garage caught on fire this morning."

"I heard," she said. We live in a very small town.

"You can still smell it."

Sara nodded. Zeno curled at her feet, resting his big hound head on her foot.

"How'd it start?" Sara said.

"They don't know. It wasn't much of a fire, really. I pretty much had it out before the guys came. Al isn't happy about it."

"Why's that?"

"I don't know. He's mad at me about it. Or about something else."

"That's not like him," Sara said. "Maybe he's just mad and is taking it out on you."

"That's a thought," I said.

We finished eating and I got up and cleaned the plates off the table. Zeno got up and followed me to the sink, hoping to get a scrap, which I never give him. Always a first time, he hopes. Sara, released from Zeno's weight, got up and cleared the leftovers from the table and put them in the fridge. She then pushed me away from the sink and did the dishes. It was like this most nights.

"You going up there tonight?" Sara said.

"I'll leave him be, I guess."

"He's that mad?"

"He's that mad."

"You want me to talk to him?" Sara would do that. She could talk to people more directly than I could sometimes, especially Al.

"Not tonight. What are you doing?"

She shrugged. It was a shrug that didn't mean she didn't know, but that it was none of my business. She finished washing the dishes, checked her phone, and then dawdled in the kitchen.

"You want me to stay in tonight?"

"You think I don't know what to do without Al around?"

"Do you?"

"I think I can figure it out."

"You think he'll be mad for long?"

"I couldn't say. Why, am I in your way? I can leave my own house, if that's what you want."

"No," Sara said. "I'm just trying to process you and Al. It's against the natural order of things, you know? You guys never fight."

"We're not fighting now. I'm not mad at him; he's mad at me. It's all him."

"You don't know why?"

"No more than the last time you brought it up five minutes ago."

"All right," Sara said. "Don't get mad at me. I was just trying to help."

Now everybody was mad. Except for Zeno. He was over on his bed, curled up and comfortable while the rest of the world was out of whack. Sara left, and I went into the living room and turned on the TV. Zeno came in and lay down on the floor, his body leaning into the couch. I scrolled aimlessly through a bunch of crap and then turned the phone off. I tried to read, but nothing could distract me from thinking about Al. I didn't really think for a minute that he was going to kill me, but you never know. We live in a world where it happens all the time, and it always seems surprising and at the same time unexceptional. Al was mad, that was for sure, angrier than I'd ever seen him, to a point that I wasn't sure who he was or what he might do. I was glad Sara was gone, but I almost wished she was here. Al wouldn't do anything with her around, I thought. But then, you can never be sure.

We live in a town where there hasn't been a murder in almost five years. But that was a murder-suicide. Brad Scheffler shot his wife and then himself. To this day they don't know why. No one thought they didn't have a good marriage, no indication of infidelity, disagreements, nothing to suggest any discord. Brad was a mechanic, served on the local planning and zoning committee, and his wife Laura was a substitute teacher who volunteered at the food pantry. They'd been married almost thirty years. Then one morning they find them both in their living room. Laura shot with a rifle and Brad shot with a pistol, both guns found near his body. There's some rumors about it, of course, but there's no reason to any of it. There never is, if you think about it. Al could walk down the hill and shoot me through the window while I'm sitting here on the couch. Or he could wait until tomorrow like he says he will and shoot me while I'm walking Zeno past his house. Or any other time, for that matter. I could call the cops, I suppose, but what would they do about it? Maybe drive down the twenty minutes from the station and ask Al a bunch of questions that would only make him angrier. Maybe they'd take his guns—I don't know—but he could easily get another one. Or kill me some other way. Stab me or poison me or choke me or run me over with his car. There's plenty of ways if he's got his mind set on it.

I sat on the couch and thought of all the ways somebody could murder me and figured for every idea I had, there had to be ten more ideas I wasn't considering. You think of enough ways that it almost seems inevitable, and then preposterous, and then inevitable again, and then round and round. I thought about Ole Anderson lying on his bed in "The Killers," waiting for the men to come. There's nothing to be done about it, he figures. I tried to remember why they were after him. I got up and went to see if I still had my collection of Hemingway stories. I didn't have that many books around the house. I'd gotten rid of most of them over the years, and my wife took some when she left. She wouldn't take Hemingway, though. It had been a hardcover; I'd picked it up at the annual library sale. People in town donate books and you see the same books there from one year to the next; somebody buys it, reads it, and donates it back so somebody else can buy it. Maybe that's what I did. Bought it, read it, and donated it back. It wasn't in the house and I couldn't remember why they were going to kill Ole Anderson. Maybe Hemingway never explained it. It didn't matter. I went back to the couch and rubbed Zeno on the back of his ears and tried not to think about Ole Anderson and what happened to my books and if my wife took it after all, and if I was really going to be murdered tomorrow.

The morning after the fire I took Zeno up the hill for our walk. The sky was orange and blue as the sun started its work for the day. It could have been any other day, but it never is. I just didn't know how different it was going to be.

We walked to Al's house and looked around. You didn't notice the fire from the road. It's funny how everything can look the same if you don't pay attention. Zeno put his nose up, sniffing at the air, taking in the story of the fire and the men who had been on the road. I let him take his time. There had been a few mornings over the past few years when Al would come out with his coffee and a treat for Zeno, and maybe a cup of coffee for me, and we'd stand around and talk. Not today. But then, that was most days. We made our way past Al's house and turned around at the "Slow Children Playing" sign that approximated a mile from my house. The sign was old; there hadn't been any children in the neighborhood since Sara was little, and that was a mile back and years ago. Zeno and I turned around and slowed when we passed Al's again. The fire could have been a lot worse. It shouldn't be too bad to clean up and get things back to normal.

When we got home, I fed Zeno and poured myself some coffee and made some eggs and toast. Zeno curled on his bed and his eyes grew heavy. He could go back to sleep; I had to get to work. I drank my coffee and stared at the toaster until black smoke started to come out of it.

That's how stuck I was on this thing with Al. I got a knife and scraped at the charred slices of bread until I gave up and started over. I'd let him ruin the toast, but that's as far as it would go. I wouldn't let him ruin everything, as much as he might want. I cleaned the dishes and rubbed Zeno's nose the way he likes and drove up to Al's. He wasn't ready, but then, he was never ready. He had a cup of coffee in his hand when he opened the door and was still in his socks. He didn't invite me in but I walked in anyway, and he walked silently in front of me and went into the kitchen and sat down like he wasn't going to move again.

Al's first wife divorced him after about a year of marriage. That was his high school girlfriend. We'd double-dated to the senior prom. She lived in the next town over, Caldwell, and I couldn't even tell you how they met. I didn't even know Al was seeing anyone until he told me he was going to the prom with her. "You should get a date," he said, "and we'll go together." So I asked one of the girls from high school who didn't have a date already. It wasn't that easy. I already had a reputation, and a lot of parents didn't want their daughters to have anything to do with me. At least, that's the way I like to look at it. Could be that I wasn't attractive enough to get a girlfriend, or even a date. Or it could be that I wasn't that interested to begin with; I was too busy trying to make easy money to think about having a girlfriend. Anyway, I asked around and finally Christi Walker said she'd go with me. We had a good enough time but we were just friends and didn't really have anything to do with each other afterward. Christi Walker ended up going to college and never talking to me again. She became a doctor in New Haven, I think. I'm not completely sure, but I followed her enough online to know that she's done all right for herself. I used to think that way about my own life too. And Al. He got married a couple of months after graduation. Thinks he rented the exact same tux for the wedding that he had at prom. "There was a mark on the tag on the jacket pocket," he said. When I told him that maybe every jacket had the same mark, he said, "Not this mark. I remember it distinctly." So he wore the same tux and got married in the summer. And divorced the next spring. She moved out to California, I think. Then Al got married again about six months later. Vera. She lived about half an hour away and met Al online. They only went out a dozen times or so and then decided to get married. I liked her. Everybody did. She was smart and funny and kept Al in line, looked after him and he looked after her. We spent a lot of time together, the four of us, for drinks, dinner, weekends, vacations. And she and my wife spent a lot of time together. Vera ran the animal shelter where we would eventually get Zeno. She'd studied to be a vet but never finished. She loved animals and had a funny explanation for why she didn't become a vet. "I love animals," she said, "I just don't love them enough to spend my life sticking my hand up their butts all day long." And she loved Al. They were married fifteen years and would still be married, I bet, but she died a few years ago from cancer. A couple of years before my wife left. Al kept her stuff around the house like maybe she was coming back, her purse was still in a chair in the living room, her makeup and pills still in the bathroom cabinet, her clothes still in the closet, a dress still over the chair in the bedroom, laid out for another day that never came. There was no trace of my wife anywhere in the house, everything had been taken to the dump, or burned. Maybe Sara has a picture or something, but that's her business and she never has it out in the open. Al lived in a museum, or a time capsule stuck on the day before his wife died. "Five years. That's what it usually takes to get over it," my wife had said. She'd been good to Al afterward, caring and comforting, spending most of her time looking out for him. He stayed with us for a few weeks after the funeral and she made a point of making sure he got fed and got distracted. She tried to make him laugh a little every day. "Five years," she said, but she didn't stick around to see if she was right. Once she left, she didn't have anything to do with Al. He never talked about her, never talked about his wife. We were like two old men with nothing but the past between us. And that's never enough.

I stood in the kitchen and watched Al drink his coffee. He didn't even look at me. "Whenever you're ready," I said and Al got up and threw the last of his coffee in the sink and put the cup down and walked down the hallway toward the door. I followed him as he grabbed his jacket and walked out onto the small porch and waited for me to get out of the house before he locked the door. He got into the passenger seat, and before I started the car I turned to him and said, "I don't think it's as bad as you think."

"What's that?"

"The fire. I don't think it's anything to worry about."

"I'm not worried about it," he said.

"We'll fix it up," I said. "I can help."

He didn't say anything and I drove off like I do most mornings when we went to work. He looked out the window, his jaw clenched and a determined coldness in his eyes; you could practically see the anger building in him.

"You want to talk about it?" I said.

"Talk about it?"

"Yeah. Whatever it is that got stuck in your craw."

"Did you shower this morning?" Al said.

"No," I said, caught off guard by his question.

"You should have."

"There's people that shower before work, and those who shower after work," I said. "I always shower after work. You know that." I made a mock motion to turn my head and sniff my right armpit. "You think I stink?"

"Like the shit you are," Al said.

"What's that supposed to mean?"

"I know you," he said. "I know who you are."

"I thought so," I said. "But maybe not. Who am I?"

Al didn't say anything. We pulled into the back of the Flying F bar and we walked to the door like we did every Thursday morning. The door was locked and Al banged on it with his fist.

"I hate when they do that," I said. "They know we're coming."

Al banged again and we stood and waited for someone to open up.

A kid we didn't know opened the door a few inches and looked at us like we were the ones who didn't belong there.

Al grabbed the door and pulled it open and said, "Where's Fitz?"

"He's not here. Who are you guys?"

"We're the guys who can get you fired if you don't take us to see Fitz," Al said.

"He's expecting us," I said. "Tell him Peck and Al are here. Like we are every week."

The kid hesitated and I thought Al might grab him and throw him out the door behind us if he didn't move out of the way, but finally the kid turned around and took us into the bar where Fitz was sitting counting his money from the night before. We went and sat at the table and Fitz waved the kid away.

"Who's that?" Al said.

"That's Roy. Some kid I have to find work for. A favor. Don't ask, don't worry. He won't be around long."

"You could have told him we were coming."

"I could have. But I didn't want to. I wanted to see how he'd handle it."

"And how'd he handle it?" I asked.

"He let you in, didn't he?"

"We came in," Al said.

"Like I said, he won't be around long. Don't worry about it."

I got up and walked toward the bar. "You got any coffee?"

"Just put it on. I can have the kid get it."

"How do I take my coffee?"

"Black, like mine," Fitz said.

"And how does Al take it?"

"With a splash of Four Roses."

"Think the kid can do that?"

"I'll see to it."

I'd already gone behind the bar and was pouring the coffee.

"I've got it," I said and brought a black coffee for Fitz and one with a splash for Al. I went to the bar and got my own, the way I did every time. I went back and sat at the table and waited.

Fitz took a bank deposit bag and handed it to me. I unzipped it and took out the money and counted it, then gave it to Al and he counted it. We both came to the same amount.

"You want the kid to show us out," Al said, "maybe see how he can handle that?"

"The way you look, I'm not sure he'd be able to make it back," Fitz said. "Be happy, Al, we had a good week."

"We. Shit. Maybe you had a good week; I know Peck had a good week, but I had a shitty week." Al reached across the table and took a stack of bills and put it in his jacket. "Maybe your week just got a little worse," he said and got up and left.

Fitz and I looked at each other, Fitz stunned and open-mouthed, and me stunned and trying not to apologize for my partner. He was out of line, but I couldn't go against him, not with Fitz.

"I don't know what set him off," I said, "But that's on you. Don't speak for him. And get rid of the kid. You should have known from the way Al was banging on the door he wasn't happy."

"The kid's gone," Fitz said. "But see that Al gets over it, will you? Talk to him, Peck."

"I'll talk to him," I said. "We'll see you next week."

I got into the car and Al was sitting in the passenger seat, steam practically come out of his jacket collar.

"What was that all about?" I said.

He didn't even know I was there.

"Are you at least going to give me some of what you took?"

"Fuck you," Al said and I drove off.

We had a few more collections to make and Al didn't say a word. In fact, he stayed in the car and everything was fine as far as the work went, but I couldn't take his foul mood anymore.

"Maybe I should drop you off back home," I said.

"Okay."

We drove back to his house in silence and instead of pulling off to the side of the road, I pulled into Al's drive. You could see the damage from the fire from there, smell the damp, charred wood and drywall. It wasn't bad. The fire department had done the worst of it. We could get it back into shape no problem. Al got out of the car and I followed him. He stopped and turned back on me like a startled animal.

"Where are you going?" he said.

"Let's have it," I said.

"I know what you did," he said.

"That makes one of us."

"I could kill you for it."

He wasn't kidding. "Okay. Calm down and tell me what's going on, Al. I don't know what I've done to piss you off so bad, but tell me and I'll make things right if I can."

He looked back toward his garage and then back at me. His eyes were still hard and pained, but not crazy like before.

"My hard drive's gone," he said.

"And you think I took it."

"It's no good to anyone else," Al said. "You're the only one who can access it."

"I didn't take it, Al. I swear to God. I would never take it. Never. Besides, I don't even know where you keep it."

He didn't believe me. "That's what the fire was all about," he said. "You knew."

"I didn't know. I don't know. Come to the house. Take a look. Tear the place down if you want. I don't have it."

"It's no good to anyone else," he said. "You've taken it somewhere."

"We'll find it. I'll help you find it."

"You're a liar," he said. "You're a cheat and a liar."

"But I'm not a thief," I said. "Not with you. I wouldn't steal from you, you know it."

"I know what I know," he said. He was still mad, but at least he didn't look like he was going to attack me there in his driveway.

"Twenty years, I've never taken a nickel from you. And I never would. Anything I've got, you can have. You know that. You know you can trust me, Al. After all we've been through . . ."

"Okay," he said and dropped his eyes from mine. He went into his house and left me standing there wondering what had happened.

There'd never been any secrets between us. We'd been friends since he moved to town more than twenty years ago, when we were both still in high school. We got into trouble almost as soon as we met.

We were walking home from school one afternoon when we saw a delivery truck open, with no driver around. Al walked to the back of the truck and grabbed a box and took off running. Without thinking, I did the same thing. We ran through some backyards and into the park nearby. The boxes were light and no trouble at all to run with. Al stopped at a bench and sat down and put the box next to him. I caught up and put the box on the bench and stood in front of him and tried to catch my breath.

"What did you get?" I asked him.

"I don't know," he said. "What did you grab?"

"I don't know." We opened the boxes. They were filled with bags of potato chips, small bags, like for a vending machine. We took them to school the next day and sold them for a quarter each, if we could get it, some for less, and some we gave away. We didn't care; anything we got was profit, and we split it fifty-fifty. That's the way it's been ever since, no matter what we took. And we've taken a lot.

I knew what was on the hard drive. Al had told me about it, even gave me his passwords and access codes. He put them in an envelope and told me to hold on to it. "Just in case," he told me. I honestly don't know where he kept it, an important piece of information he never told me. It didn't matter; I only had the envelope for an emergency, like if Al lost all his information. "You're the only person I can trust," he told me, but that was a long time ago and things have apparently changed. I put the envelope in the safe in the basement and didn't give it another thought. Honestly. Al was never going to need it; he was better with all that stuff than I was, more careful, more conscientious. No one was going to get between Al and his money. Or so I thought. I also figured that he had a backup, but I was wrong, and now there was one code he was particularly concerned about, and it was worth a couple of million dollars.

Al had put some of his money into cryptocurrency back in the early days, and he'd opened accounts at a number of exchanges. But he was always suspicious of anything online, believed it was susceptible to hackers, scammers, fraudsters. He kept investing in crypto but moved everything offline, taking all of it out of the hot wallets and exchanges and parking it on his hard drive. "You can't beat air for a security shield," he said, waving his hand in a circle around his drive. "If it's unplugged, it's untouched." He wrapped the cord around the small drive and then put it in his safe. Whenever he wanted to get at it, the only way he could access the stuff was with a specific password that's impossible to memorize, so he wrote it down and kept a copy for himself and gave me one. After a number of high-value hacks like the Ronin Network and Wormhole, and the collapse of FTX, Al felt vindicated, but now that his hard drive has gone missing, he thinks I've stolen it all from him.

I would have liked to have figured out what to do about Al and his missing fortune right then, but I had work to do.

I went down to the Flying F like I did most mornings, Monday through Friday. Al only went with me on Thursdays. Zeno went with me some of the time. I should have taken him more, maybe, or less, I'm not sure. Fitz was nervous around Zeno, though he tried to fake that he wasn't by bringing him treats and talking to him in what he thought was a soothing voice from a far distance. Zeno could get a hard look about him, that watchful, wary, intimidating look a German shepherd can have, with his dark eyes fixed on you. Whenever someone asked if Zeno was friendly I always gave the same reply: "When I want him to be."

I don't want people around Zeno all that much; you never know what they're going to do, what food they're going to give him or how they're going to handle him. I also try to remember that he's Sara's dog and I want him to protect her, or at least have people think he can. Having a big dog that people have to wonder about isn't a bad thing. So I didn't want Fitz nervous around Zeno, but I didn't do a lot to discourage it. I'd bring Zeno into the bar and be a little amused when Zeno would give Fitz a hard, watchful stare. Let Zeno act like he ran the place.

I don't own the Flying F anymore, but I still work there, do the books, take care of the deposits, make sure everything is running the way it should. Nothing's changed, really, except I get a paycheck and the bar's not in my name. If I had to do it again, I don't know that I would have sold it, but extreme circumstances sometimes demand extreme measures. I'm not going to go into the whole thing, but when I found out my wife was leaving me, leaving me for someone else, I sold the place to Fitz and hid the money from my wife. Al helped me figure out a lot of it, trusts, LLCs, offshore accounts, foreign transfers, even Al held on to some accounts for a short time. We went through lawyers and accountants in the end, to make it all legal, but it was Al who did the real work. The rest of them just put it down on paper. Sara would get it all, but the ex wouldn't see a nickel. Let the new guy take care of her. Let him try.

I let myself in—Al always insisted on banging on the door ("Make them get off their asses for a minute and come and greet us," he said)—and Fitz was sitting at the bar, talking on the phone. He ended his call when he saw me. I walked behind the bar and Zeno found a spot under a table and curled up.

"You got any coffee on?" I said.

"Should be ready just now," he said, and texted something and put his phone face down on the bar. "Let the kid get it for you." He looked around but didn't see him.

"I got it," I said. "I always get the coffee. You want some?"

"Sure," Fitz said.

"Black?"

"You always ask. It's always the same, black."

"I always ask. That's why you're good at this and I'm not." I poured us both a cup and put his in front of him. I took mine down to the end of the bar and started working on the books. After a while the kid showed his face and Fitz waved him off. The kid went somewhere else and grabbed a broom and probably took a long while to figure out how to work it. I could hear work starting in the kitchen. That was a whole different universe. They had their own entrance, their own manager, their own way of doing things. I always left them alone. Fitz wandered back, "You want anything?" he asked. "Some eggs or something." They'd be working hard enough to get ready for lunch, they didn't need to waste time on me. I shook my head and went back to the books.

Fitz came back after a while with some bread and butter and a paper plate with peanut butter smeared on it. He set the plate down and Zeno got up and went to work on the peanut butter, happier than anyone else in the place, maybe happier than anyone else in the state. Fitz poured himself another cup of coffee and ate his bread and looked at his phone.

"You like mulligatawny soup?" Fitz asked.

"I think so. I like most soups, though, I guess."

"I suggested to the kitchen that they make it this month, you know, St. Patrick's and all. They about laughed me out of the place."

"You thought it was Irish."

"I thought it was Irish stew or something."

"It's not, I take it," I said.

"Indian. I thought they were kidding me. Mulligatawny. Sounds Irish to me. I had to look it up."

"Indian?"

"Indian. Sounds Irish, tastes Indian."

"I still like it," I said.

"Not this month," Fitz said. He finished his coffee and pushed the cup away from him. "I should travel more. You too, Peck."

Fitz was like me, his family had been here for generations, most of them buried not far from where they were born.

"We never leave, do we?"

"If we did, the whole place would go to shit before we came back," Fitz said.

"We'll let the kid run it," I said.

"He'll be all right," Fitz said. "I need to head out for a minute." He went and grabbed the deposit bag.

"I need to go to the bank," I said. "Want me to take it?" Fitz handed me the bag and I left.

I handed over the bag, and the teller counted it and handed me the receipt. "Where's Fitz?" she said.

"Not here is about as much as I know," I said. The teller smiled. She'd known me a long time. She'd rather see Fitz. Fitz would give her a conversation, give her something to pass the time or interest her, maybe even talk to her about soup.

"You need any change?"

"We're good," I said. "And if I'm wrong, I'll send Fitz back."

"You won't be wrong," she said and sounded a little disappointed.

I walked over to the service area, where one of the managers was seated.

"He in?" I said, nodding to a closed door in the corner.

She picked up the phone and spoke and then said to me, "He'll be just a minute. You want to wait?"

I nodded and took a chair.

When I was little, we'd come to the bank on Saturday mornings—always Saturday mornings—and my grandmother would park me in a seat and she'd go behind the same closed door and do some transaction or other. She never had much money, and I don't know what she did in there, but they always treated her like she had a million bucks, I remember that. She'd always give me a book to read, and I'd sit and wait and try to concentrate on the words on the page, but I couldn't help but always look toward the vault, and the room where they kept the safety-deposit boxes, and the tellers counting the money. My grandmother liked her crime novels—she typically left me with an Agatha Christie when she made her bank visits—*The Mysterious Affair at Styles*, *Five Little Pigs*, *Three Act Tragedy*, stuff like that. Maybe she thought that trying to solve a mystery would distract me from all that money. It did not. And maybe not my grandmother either—she always liked a good crime movie, and I remember watching *Loose Change* with her as a kid. She took me to the movies to see it, I remember, a Saturday matinee. And I remember watching *The Thomas Crown Affair* and *Thunderbolt and Lightfoot* and *Dog Day Afternoon* with her on TV. Maybe she knew what I was thinking all those Saturday mornings sitting there in the bank and not reading the books she gave me. Maybe she wanted to disabuse me of any ideas I might have about pulling a heist. Or maybe she just liked good movies. Whatever she liked, I liked too. I just took it all more to heart.

Rick Holley emerged from his office and waved me toward him and I got up and walked toward his flapping hand.

"What can I do for you today?" he said and his hand waved toward an empty chair.

"I wanted to ask you about a home equity loan," I said.

"Can I ask why a home equity loan? I mean, there might be a better solution depending on what you need."

"I'm not sure," I said, "but I think I might need a fair amount of money here soon, and I thought maybe a home equity loan could cover some of it."

"How much money?"

"Maybe two million."

"You're not going to buy back the bar, are you?"

"Not for two million, no, if that's what you're worried about."

"Well, if you get it back, maybe you could change the name."

"A rose by any other name," I said.

"What's that?"

"I think it's Shakespeare, but you're the one who went to college."

"Business school," Rick said.

“Well, you get what you pay for.”

Rick took me through a few different options, from home equity to HELOC to taking a line of credit. I can do the books at the bar and keep track of the cash as it comes in and goes out, but this is where my grasp of it ends. I’m fine with cash; I have a harder time with interest rates and revolving credit and all that other stuff. He had me confused, none of it his fault, except I could see we weren’t going to get where I wanted, not easily, anyway.

“The problem is,” he said, “you have most of your assets tied up in your trust.”

“It’s not my trust,” I said. “That’s Sara’s.”

“I know. Sorry. Anyway, I think we can get you close. When will you know the exact amount and when you’ll need it?”

“I may not need it,” I said. “I just wanted to be prepared.”

“Maybe your brother could cosign something. Have you thought of that?”

“Yeah. That’s not an option. And if you see him, I wasn’t here.”

“Understood. I’m here to help.”

“I appreciate it.”

“You want me to get to work on anything? I can get the paperwork in order, and if you need it, we can move on it, if not, that’s fine too.”

“Give me a couple of days,” I said. “I’m jumping the gun a little, I guess. I’ll know more in a couple of days.”

“That’s fine too. How’s everything?”

“Everything’s good.”

“How’s Sara?”

“Adultlike.”

“I heard she was driving. I didn’t know she turned sixteen.”

“Last month. She’s not happy with the car I gave her.”

“You gave her yours. I did the same thing.”

"What was your first car?"

"My parents gave me a brand-new Ford Mustang. I totaled it three months later. I think I remember yours. It was your grandmother's Bonneville."

"Big Black, everybody called it, remember?"

"Not when she was around," Rick said. "She was such a nice person."

"The black sheep of the family," I said.

I walked to the car and got Zeno, who was curled up in the back seat, and got him out and took him for a walk. Rick must have put me in a nostalgic mood, or maybe I was getting that way on my own. I looked at the storefronts and only saw the businesses from my childhood, the bookstore, the toy store, the pet store, the shoe store, clothing store, drug store, even the fabric store where I would almost go crazy waiting for my grandmother as she went through bolt after bolt of fabric looking for the right pattern for the new curtains, a new dress, clothes she'd make for newborns in town. All of those businesses were gone now. There were too many empty storefronts, and too many restaurants, mostly chains. The mom -and -pops that were struggling before the pandemic got pounded and most of them didn't make it. I'd sold the Flying F before that and Fitz thought I left him holding the bag for a while, but he did all right in the end. He figured out how to get food out the door and I figured out how to keep the operation running. Fitz even got money from the government. If it had been me, the place probably would have gone under.

Zeno and I went back to the car and drove to the south edge of town to the hardware store. I took Zeno with me. He'd be happy to see Al, if he was there. He wasn't. I did see Fitz, however, buying parts for a broken toilet.

"You want me to take care of that?" I said.

"I'm hoping to make it better, not worse," he said. Fitz wandered the aisles, picking up a few more items along the way. He wouldn't pay for any of it, just stopped at the counter long enough to give instructions. "Make sure Al knows I was here," he told the cashier.

Zeno and I wandered back to Al's office but he didn't look as if he'd been around all day. I wasn't going to text him; I wasn't sure what I would have said to him if I'd seen him. I wanted him to know that I wasn't avoiding him. Maybe I should have been.

After dinner, after Zeno and Sara had gone off to her room, I gave Al a call and tried to calm things. It didn't go well.

"Can't you access your account some other way?" I asked him.

"I'm going to kill you tomorrow."

"I don't have it, Al. If you think about it, you'll know that I don't have it. Because I'd never take it, and if I ever did, I'd give it right back. I don't want your money. I don't want anything. In fact, if you want money, I'll give you everything I've got. How about that?"

"You don't have any money," he said. "And you betrayed me."

"I wouldn't."

"You did. I never thought that would happen, but it did. It has."

"It has not. Absolutely, one hundred percent not true."

"Maybe not yet, then. But it's going to."

"Under no circumstances."

"Maybe to save your own neck. Or Sara's."

"What does she have to do with it?"

"You should ask her."

"I'm asking you, Al."

Al didn't say anything. I thought maybe he wanted to tell me but was hesitating. I didn't want to jump in too early and push him away, but I didn't want to give him enough time to think himself out of telling me.

I let him hesitate for a while, and then said, "If you kill me, promise me one thing."

"What's that?"

"That you'll take care of Sara. And Zeno."

"You don't think Sara will want nothing to do with me?"

"That's up to her. But you, you have to promise to take care of her."

"I promise," he said. And I believed him. I really did.

"Is she in trouble? Can you tell me that?"

"I don't know." More silence. "This is what I know. They're coming for you. Extortion. You need to come up with a lot of money. That's why you took the hard drive."

"I wouldn't steal it from you. I'd ask you for the money. You know that."

"And I'd give it to you. But not this time. Maybe that's part of it. You had to take it. That was part of the deal."

"I'd tell you what was going on. Because if they're coming for me they're coming for you next."

"Not this time," Al said. "They're only coming for you."

"Who is?"

"Somebody working with your ex," Al said.

"I haven't talked to my ex in three years. You know that."

"She's talking to Sara," he said.

"This doesn't make any sense, Al."

"Not the way you're looking at it. I'm telling you what I know."

"Well, I don't know any of it. I swear."

"I'd like to believe you, but I can't. Because you can't tell me what you know. You can't say anything about it."

"I'll figure this out. Promise me you won't do anything until I've got some time to figure this out. Someone's talking shit to tear us apart."

“Maybe that’s how you see it. But I’m the one missing a drive that can only be accessed by you. That’s how I see it.”

“Okay. But at least don’t kill me until I can figure out what’s going on.”

“We’ll see,” Al said. “This is a crazy way to go about this, though, isn’t it?”

“It’s the only thing that makes sense in the whole cockeyed world, Al.”

I opened my eyes, more tired than when I'd closed them. I looked at my watch, expecting the time to have inched forward a minute or two, and was surprised that two hours had passed. Sometimes it's worse to get a little sleep than none at all. I put my head back on the pillow and then thought better of it. I got out of bed quickly, trying to leave the groggy tiredness behind and went downstairs. Zeno raised his head and watched me walking past, but then put his head down and went back to sleep. Zeno had better sense. I went into the kitchen and drank a glass of water and stood by the back door and looked out into the dark. There were animals, I thought, moving out there, living their lives in the darkness. Raccoons, possums, skunks, deer, who knows what else, walking through the yard, eating grass, plants, going after the garden in a few months, using it as a giant buffet, and a toilet. People said they'd seen coyotes on the golf course nearby. I'd never seen them, but sometimes heard them howling—happy, almost mocking howls off in the distance. Maybe they were celebrating. One morning I found a decapitated rabbit in the yard. Everything intact, but the head completely missing. "Most likely a cat," Al had told me. "You can almost be sure of it." I'd never seen a cat around, and thought Zeno would go nuts over a cat in the yard. "Maybe a hawk, then," Al said. "But just because you haven't seen a cat doesn't mean one isn't there." Sometimes Zeno would bark at night, at something only he could see, or hear, or sense, something beyond my abilities to notice. Now I studied the darkness but didn't see anything moving. Maybe they knew I was there. I wasn't entirely awake but couldn't go back to sleep. I was thinking about Al.

I had to figure out how to put things right. But how can you do that when someone refuses to listen to reason, when someone clings to their own version of the truth? There had to be more to it than Al was letting on. You don't throw over a friend and partner that easy, do you? Maybe there'd been trouble for a long time, trouble I didn't see, like animals moving around in the dark, doing their damage right in front of me but I didn't notice, didn't have the ability to see it all turning bad.

I drank another glass of water and decided to go back upstairs and get dressed. I passed Sara's room on the way and looked in to check on her. Her bed was empty. I went and sat in the armchair in my room and stared into the dark. I could see Zeno's eyes shining as he watched me. I called him over and he came and sat next to me and put his large head on my knee, and I scratched between his ears and eyes and down his nose. When I stopped, he flicked his head underneath my hand to let me know to start again. After a while I started to nod off, and Zeno lay down at my feet and I must have slept a little.

When I woke again it was morning, and I went to the safe I had in the back of the closet, a small thing no bigger than a minibar fridge you find in a hotel, and opened it and got the envelope out of it and put it in my pocket. I took Zeno for a walk up the hill. I went past Al's but didn't see him. Zeno marked a spot near the road where a truck had leaked some oil. I was sort of hoping he'd take a shit in Al's yard, but Zeno wasn't spiteful like that. We walked past the house and then turned around and went back home. I kept the envelope in my pocket.

I fed Zeno and then had my own breakfast and checked Sara's room. Still empty. I texted her and didn't get anything back. It wasn't time to worry yet. It was too early for her to be awake. I had another cup of coffee and scrolled through the news. Nothing important, nothing that was going to change my life one way or the other. What I needed to do was get back up the hill. I sat and wondered how much more stalling I was going to do before I actually did it. You have to approach it just right, even with someone you've known for a couple of decades. I let the coffee go cold and threw it down the sink, then did the dishes, washed and dried everything and put them back where they should be. Then I gave Zeno a good rub on his nose the way he likes and left.

I drove up the hill and parked the car and knocked on the back door like I'd done hundreds of times on hundreds of mornings just like this one. Al came to the door like he does, his coffee in his hand and his shoes off, as if he's not expecting me.

"You want to go or do you want to talk about it?" I said.

"Whichever way you want," he said.

"I didn't take it," I told him again and handed him back the envelope.

It had never been opened. Al could see that.

"Could be a different envelope," he said.

His own handwriting was still on it. "Peck—just in case," he'd written in small, scratchy letters that no one could imitate.

"Doesn't matter anyway," Al said. "Maybe you just got caught before you could open the envelope. Besides, once you've got the drive, you can wait it out."

It was pointless. Al had gone crazy, or he was going to drive me crazy. Either he was going to kill me or would drive me to kill him. Or nothing. We would wait for it, but it would never happen, like Didi and Gogo or, worse, Lucky and Pozzo. I couldn't prove to him that I didn't have it. The only thing to do was to help find it.

"So what do you want to do?" I said.

"Let's go to work."

Sara texted me. "Over at Kelly's." That was helpful, but didn't really put me at ease. There were two Kellys in Sara's class. One was a boy I hoped she wasn't sleeping with, and the other was a girl, who I guess I also hoped she wasn't sleeping with. Sara was at the age where her sexuality and decisions were her own business, but I was at the age where I hoped she wasn't making any decisions or doing any business of her own. It was a predicament I tried to keep to myself.

About two weeks after my wife left, Sara said she wanted a dog. She was depressed, despondent, and angry, and rightfully so. She'd always wanted one, but now she was practically demanding one. I didn't want one, but took her to the animal shelter anyway. We had agreed on a set of criteria before we went. The dog had to be an adult (no puppies!); they had to be house-trained; they had to be calm and well-behaved; they had to be relatively low energy; and they could not shed or slobber everywhere. Sara went online and found a few candidates at the shelter. But there was no other option than Zeno. He and Sara bonded almost immediately. When they opened his cage for us to meet him, Zeno ran to Sara and didn't want to leave, and Sara didn't want to leave him.

He was about a year old, greyhound and German shepherd mix, the shelter thought. And that's exactly what he looked like: short brown coat, deep chest with a long tail, and a dark face that was full and long. "He'll need long walks," they told us. "And he does shed." We took him home. He was going to be Sara's dog. She was going to take care of him, walk him and feed him and clean up after him. I started walking him after the first month, started feeding him after the second month, and seemed to be always cleaning up after him. He still runs to Sara the minute he sees her and sleeps in her room most nights. He's still her dog, I'm just the one who takes care of his every need.

When I tell people that his name is Zeno, invariably someone tells me that "You should never put a command in the name, like 'no.' You use it all the time and they won't be able to differentiate between the name and the command. You're confusing the dog every time." First, don't ever tell me what to do with our dog. Second, we didn't give Zeno any name. That's the name he came with. I asked Sara if she wanted to change it, and she didn't. He already knew his name, and Sara liked it. Third, she hardly calls him Zeno anyway. It's always Z-Dog, or Z-Boy, Z-Man, Z-Nog, Z-Noggin, or my least favorite, Z-Bub, which Sara likes to tell people is short for Beelzebub. Sara has raised Zeno to be a sweet dog, but she says, "It doesn't hurt to make people think twice about it. Make them think maybe we've got a good guard dog." Zeno wouldn't guard his own food bowl. But he listens to Sara and has seen her through tough times. Fourth, no one ever knows what the hell they're talking about.

There were five houses completed in the subdivision when Al and I bought out here, a half dozen more scattered along the road in various stages of progress. Three of the completed houses were already under contract. We liked the remaining two equally, and I let Al pick which one he wanted. He wanted to be on the top of the hill. I was happy to have a house anywhere. I never thought we'd make it that far, owning a house, getting married, having a family. I always figured I'd wind up in prison before any of that happened. But here we were, homeowners in our twenties, Al married and me about to be. Once it had been a life we could never imagine for ourselves, now we had it and stupidly thought it would stay that way forever. Of course it didn't. Nothing stays the same. Happiness never lasts. You know it's a fact, maybe even a law, like physics or something, but then you're still surprised when the big changes come. Cancer, divorce, death. Betrayal.

About a week after we stole the potato chips, Al and I were walking home from school again and a delivery truck suddenly sped up and raced toward us. Al and I took off running. The truck stopped and the driver got out and chased after us. Al was faster than I was that day and I could feel the driver gaining on me. There was nothing I could do about it; I was running as fast as I could and the guy was getting closer and closer. Then I felt him grab me by the back of my shirt and pull me down. I hit the ground and the guy landed on top of me. I could see Al slowing down, looking back at us. "Go," I yelled at him, but he didn't. He came back. He could have gotten away, but he came back. You don't forget that. Not ever.

"Why didn't you keep running?" I asked him later. "You could have gotten away."

"Let me ask you this," Al said. "If I hadn't grabbed that box off the truck first, would you have grabbed it?"

"Probably not," I said. I was a follower then. If Al hadn't made the first move, the idea would have never entered my mind.

"That's why I stopped."

We were partners from then on, no matter what.

I'm going to jump in here. I found these pages my dad's been writing, and just need to call out some stuff. Aren't we all sick of bromance? Why is it that the male bond gets used and overused all the time? It's a cliché. But it's also true. My dad and Al are inseparable, have been most of their lives. They've spent more of their lives together than with anyone else—more than their wives, children, pets, any other friends. They live near each other, work together, and when they're not working, they're hanging out with each other. It's disgusting how close they are. And it's sad. Until now. Al's gone crazy, except not entirely. And my father is clueless, but not as much as he'd like you to think.

I started looking at his little manuscript here to try and clean it up, to take out anything that might get him in trouble. He needs protecting, and not just from Al. There are people who are after my father, but not necessarily the ones he thinks, or the ones Al's telling him. My dad is telling too much, maybe, and not enough.

Like about the bromance. My father and Al love each other like brothers. Because they are brothers. I don't know why he's not telling you that. They have the same mother and different fathers. Al was born thirteen months after my dad, but they grew up apart, different towns and no one said anything until Grandma moved back with Al when he was fifteen. They've been together nonstop almost since then. Brothers. I don't know why he's leaving that out. Maybe he thought it was too Biblical. You know, Cain and Abel, Ishmael and Isaac, Esau and Jacob. Aaron and Moses, David and Eliab, even Absalom and Solomon. It's not a great book for brothers. Or maybe he thought it was too musical, the Louvins, the Everlys, the Davies, the Gallaghers. Not a great history there either. Maybe he didn't want to tip his hand too early; maybe he would have gotten around to it later and was just trying to build some suspense, throw in a twist or reveal when things start to drag. Anyway, you should know about it; it's important. I hope that helps things make more sense.

Coming back from Kelly's I pulled into Al's drive, and by the time I got to the door he was already standing there waiting for me. He opened the door and I walked into the house and said right out, "Stop telling Dad that you're going to kill him. We both know that you're not."

"I'm not so sure about that."

Al walked into the living room and turned off the TV and sat on the couch. I took a chair and looked back at him. He was my uncle, my second father almost. And while my dad couldn't understand why Al was so angry, I could. I knew why he was mad, and partly it was my fault.

"What are you sure about?" I said.

"Your dad's done something he shouldn't have," he said. "He knows what he's done and I know it. And that's all I'll say about it. The rest is between me and him."

"You're wrong," I said. "I don't know where you've got your information, but it's one hundred percent wrong. Dad didn't take your hard drive—and yeah, I know about it, and not from Dad, because he wouldn't betray you in any way, ever. Doesn't have it, and doesn't know what happened to it or where it is. I know this for a fact. So stop threatening the one person who wants to help you and think about what you're doing."

"What do you know about it?"

"Just what I told you. But I've heard some talk about why you're worried about that drive."

"And where'd you hear that?"

"You forget that I go to school with all the kids of the people you work with, the cops, even the district attorney. They know things maybe even you don't."

"Maybe," he said. He leaned back into the couch and thought about it. "Do you know who took it?"

"I don't."

"Do you know what's on the hard drive?"

"I do not."

"Do you know what kind of trouble I'm in?"

"I don't."

"Then what makes you so sure about anything?"

"I'm only sure that Dad doesn't have anything to do with it. You know it too, if you'd stop long enough to think about it."

"I don't know what to think. But I can't see who else it could be."

"It's not Dad. He's too close to you to do that."

"Isn't it always the people who are closest to you that hurt you the most? They're the only ones who can."

"Now you're talking about Grandma," I said.

"She kept a lot of secrets, lied to us a long time."

"Why do you suppose that is?"

"I don't know. Everybody lets you down in the end. I know that much. But she was not a good person. You know that."

"I know that from you," I said. "Dad doesn't talk about her much."

"She's the one that called him Peck, you know."

"I didn't know that. I always figured it was you who gave him that."

My uncle shook his head. "He was Peck when I met him. Your grandmother started that when he was little, maybe from the start. She thought he looked just like Gregory Peck. Nobody else saw the resemblance, but she insisted on it. You ever see his baby picture?"

"I have."

"You think he looked like Gregory Peck?"

"He looks like a little old man, I guess, thin-faced and serious, but I don't know. I don't see it."

"Your grandmother did, or says she did. Maybe it was wishful thinking on her part. It was never true, but she kept calling him Peck until it stuck."

"The name stuck, but she didn't."

"That's right," he said. "But I wouldn't be here if she had, you know?"

"And what did she call you?"

"She always called me by the name my father gave me, Alejandro."

Every Friday we had to take a ride. We always took Al's car. There's a reason for that. Al has the same car he's had for almost the past twenty years, a Ford Explorer. It's not much to look at, but Al made some precautionary adjustments to it, which every Friday gave some peace of mind.

We would make our collections on Thursday and I'd put it all in a safe I had installed in the basement. Not a little one like I kept upstairs, but a serious bank-worthy type, fireproof and waterproof, stuck in a hunk of concrete in the back corner of the basement where no one should ever be. It's even got a camera on it, just in case. Not even the mice in the basement go near it. From Thursday night until Friday morning it has more cash in it than Al and I make in a year, but none of it is ours. Our job is to drive it about an hour into the city and hand it over, fresh and clean like new laundry. We don't ask where it's going after that, and we're never told. It's not our business.

On Friday mornings I'll take Zeno up the hill on our walk and then stop at Al's and drive the Explorer back to my house and load the cash in a special cargo container Al installed himself under the back seats. You wouldn't notice it unless you were looking for it. It's flush with the interior floor and barely visible from underneath. It's got a lock on it and Al and I are the only ones with a key. There's a strip of carpeting that goes over the top and when you put the seats in place it is absolutely invisible. I feed Zeno and go to the safe and transfer the cash to the compartment in the Explorer. Al likes to sleep in, so I let him and when I'm ready I pour us both some coffee in a couple of travel mugs and drive back up the hill and honk the horn and wait for him. I always drive.

You might be wondering why Al even goes along, but he wants to go into the city once a week. And he's required to go. The man we bring the cash to wants to see us both. He wants to count his money in front of us and look us in the eye and maybe have us stand there and recognize the fact that we are only delivery boys. Maybe he wants to remind us both that what we see, what we touch, what we carry is not ours. I know that. Al knows that. We know what to take and what to leave alone. So we stand around until the count is complete, then we go out for breakfast and maybe drive around until he gets sick of the traffic and we are glad that we live where we do. Then we drive back to my house and I get out of the Explorer and Al drives home.

"I'll see you later," I tell him, and I almost always do. It's been that way for a lot of Fridays. We never take it for granted.

I put the money in the compartment and put a couple of metal cases, small suitcases, really, into the back and went to get Al. He got into the passenger seat and I handed him his travel mug and drove off. It had been over a week since Al had threatened to kill me, but it still wasn't behind us. The mood in the Explorer was different, a distance greater than the width of the cabin, a surly silence in the passenger seat that preoccupied me and distracted me when I should have been paying attention.

"Where do you want to eat today?" I said.

"I don't care."

"Anything else you want to do when we're in town?"

"Not really."

"This the way it's going to be from now on?"

Al didn't say anything but opened a small bottle of whiskey and poured some in his travel mug and put it back in the cup holder. He tossed the bottle onto one of the back seats and looked out the window. At least I thought he was looking out the window, watching the landscape change from town to countryside, the hills flattening out to greening fields and houses dotting the roadsides at greater and greater distances. He might have been looking at the side mirror. He might have been spending all of his time contemplating the message they put there: "Objects in mirror are closer than they appear." I watched Al, glancing back to the road in front of me every few seconds, but keeping my mind on Al. He didn't say anything. He could have told me. He should have said something, and by the time I noticed it was too late to do anything about it.

Maybe he was as surprised as I was by the police car pulling up behind us, flashing its lights and wanting us to pull over.

I watched the cop come out of the driver's side door and the other one get out of the passenger side. The driver walked toward us, and the other one stayed behind the open passenger door. He was hidden from view, but you could tell he had his hand on his pistol. I looked at Al, and he was fidgeting in his seat.

"No worries," I said and I was dumb enough not to be worried at all.

The cop came up to my window and I rolled it down, and he took a step back and said, "Out of the vehicle."

I opened the door and reflexively showed him my empty hands, and Al got out of the passenger side and the cop directed us both to walk to the back of the Explorer.

"Where are you headed?" the cop said.

"Just headed into the city for the day," I said.

"What are you doing there?"

I shrugged. "What's the situation here?"

"Are you driving under the influence this morning?"

"I'm not," I said. I hadn't done anything to suggest that I had been, hadn't been speeding, hadn't swerved into a different lane, hadn't done anything.

The cop looked into the back seat and saw the bottle.

"I see an open container visible in the vehicle," he said. "I'm going to need to search the vehicle." He instructed us to move away from the Explorer and Al and I walked a few yards away. The other cop kept his eyes stuck to us as he walked toward us.

The first cop opened the doors of the Explorer facing the ditch and looked around and said, "What's in these cases?"

"Nothing," I told him.

"I'm going to take a look," he said. "Are they locked?"

"Not that I know," I said.

The cop opened one and then the other and found exactly what I told him would be in them, nothing. Then he started scrounging around, running his hands on the back of the seats and around the floorboards like some sort of foreplay. I didn't look at Al because I knew the second cop was watching us the whole time. The first cop dropped the seats down and was studying the floor for a long time. Then he grabbed a strip of carpeting and gave it a tug, exposing the long steel lid.

"You got a key for this?" he said.

"You got a warrant?" Al said.

"I've got probable cause," the cop said. "Open container. I don't need a warrant. Let's see a key."

"I need to go into my pocket," I told the cop standing near us. He nervously put his hand back onto the butt of his holstered pistol and watched me while I fished out the key from my pants. I handed him the key and he dropped it into the grass and as he bent to pick it up his head was just about the height of my right knee. I fantasized about that knee smashing into his face, but I stood there still and quiet and he picked up the key and took it to his partner. They opened the lid and Al and I stood there near the ditch as the cars passed us on the road, the drivers rubbernecking and the lights flashing and I tried to get a good view of the cops but couldn't and wanted to see Al's face too, but he had his head down, turned away from the road unless somebody he knew recognized him. They all know his Explorer anyway. Besides, we were doing nothing wrong.

After a few minutes the cops came back and the first one said, "You can go," and then they went back to their car, taking the key with them. Al and I got back into his Explorer and didn't say anything. The cops sat there and watched us.

The seats were back in place and the lid closed and the carpet strip velcroed back down, and you wouldn't know that anyone had felt up the vehicle, molested it like horny assholes. I pulled out into the road and watched their car follow us for a mile or so and then turn around.

"You know those guys?" I said.

"No. You?"

"No. But I'm going to find out who they are."

"What are we going to tell [illegible]?"

"What are you going to tell him?"

"I guess we tell him the truth," Al said. "That the cops took it."

"He won't care about that. He only cares about the money. What are we going to do about that?"

"I don't know," Al said.

"Well, you'd better figure it out," I said. "You're the one that likes a little whiskey on Friday mornings. You're the one who had to throw the bottle on the seat so they could see it. What are you going to say?"

Al didn't say anything.

Potato Chip Guy had been on the ground, holding me down by my shirt collar, and when I tried to shake him loose, he popped me on the side of my head. It hurt enough that I stopped struggling and the guy was looking me straight in the eyes when Al came flying in, barreling into the guy's head with his entire body and knocking him off of me. I guess the guy figured that Al had kept running. Now he was on the ground and Al was on top of him, beating him with one punch after another. I joined in and started kicking the guy, aiming for his stomach and his crotch. One of us got him good and he snapped into the fetal position on the ground, struggling to get some air into his lungs. Al kicked him in the small of the back and we took off running.

Al thought we were done with it.

"He knows what we look like," I said.

"He's not going to do anything," Al said, and he was sort of right. The driver didn't do anything, except to have someone else come after us.

I was in homeroom when a note came and said I needed to go to the office. There was a guy standing there who said I needed to go with him for questioning about a robbery and assault. "I don't know anything about it," I said.

"I just need you to come with me to clear this up," the man said.

I looked to the office assistant for help, but she dropped her head back to the work she was ignoring a second earlier.

"Let me call my father first," I said, even though I didn't have one to call.

"You can call him in a minute," the man said and grabbed my arm and squeezed it until it hurt. He started walking and I started walking with him before I realized we were leaving. I suppose I could have made him drag me out of the school, but I think he would have gotten me out of there one way or another. It was his only job and he wasn't going to walk out the door without me.

We walked to a car idling at the curb and when he opened the door to the back seat, Al was already inside. "I didn't even get to homeroom," he said. He looked at the guy holding my arm and said, "I'm going to need a note when we come back."

We were driven down to a warehouse near the river, an old industrial building that had been turned into offices. We went inside and were led into an office where some other guy was sitting behind a desk and Potato Chip Guy was sitting in a chair off to the side.

"You owe us some money," the man behind the desk said.

"We don't owe anybody anything," Al said.

"You owe us around five hundred dollars for the boxes you took from one of my trucks," the man said.

"We didn't take any boxes," Al said.

"We're not going to argue what isn't true," the man said. "You took the boxes. You were brave enough to do that, at least be brave enough to admit it."

"It wasn't five hundred dollars' worth," I said.

"That's the restitution. You can either pay it in cash, or you can work it off."

We didn't have the money. We probably didn't have fifty bucks between us, let alone five hundred. "What kind of work?" I said. And that's how it started.

We did whatever Potato Chip Guy told us. We loaded boxes onto the truck for delivery, mostly. Potato chips, corn chips, pretzels, that kind of crap. We did that after school and on weekends. We were low-level stock boys and we didn't even get paid for the first month, still working off the boxes we'd taken, working them off well past what it was worth.

"Lousy training for a career at FedEx," Al said. It was monotonous work, but it wasn't mindless. The boxes pretty much looked the same to us, but they all had to be in a special order, which was more difficult than it seemed. There was a system to it, boxes had to be stacked in a specific arrangement. Al and I both noticed right away that lots of the boxes were heavier than they should be.

"Not potato chips," Al would say, handing me a particularly heavy box. We didn't ask questions, and we didn't make mistakes. We did that for a month, then at the end of one day Potato Chip Guy came into the small warehouse where we worked and handed us a six -pack of beer. "Congratulations," he said, "You're all settled." We opened the beer and drank it and he said, "You've done shit work and you didn't complain. If you want to continue to do some more work, I can promise that one day it won't be shit work and that starting tomorrow, you'll get paid." We stayed.

We moved from loading trucks to going out on deliveries, and then when he felt like we knew the route and the boxes that went where, he let us drive the truck. Or, I should say, Al drove the truck and I made the deliveries. Sometimes he got out of the truck and helped. We knew all the places in town and all the people who worked there, and the deliveries were always awkward in the beginning, an unacknowledged illicit transaction where boxes were always delivered to back rooms, basements, outbuildings, anywhere that probably wasn't the best place for bags of retail snacks. We didn't ask questions and we didn't make mistakes.

It was the right approach. Potato Chip Guy approached us and said, "You can keep your mouth shut," and decided to show us what we were really doing. He trusted us enough to start packing boxes, and—just as we thought—most of them were not filled with chips. Some had drugs, we think, and some had prescription drugs, bottles and bottles of them, and some had cash. We had to empty out the chips and put the new contents in the bag and reseal them. We had to put special marks on them, subtle, almost undetectable imprints, in order to tell them apart from the regular stuff. Then we had to keep track of everything and know where it went and to whom. The drugs went to dealers, we think, and the prescription stuff went to the pharmacy, and the cash went to a lot of places. The bar now known as the Flying F took a lot of boxes, and the hardware store. The hardware store had a small rack of chips off in a corner and I bet they sold a couple of bags a month. We were sending them almost ten boxes a day. You don't learn that stuff at FedEx, at least I don't think you do.

We hated it at first, especially seeing all that cash go through our fingers. We had to keep track of every last cent, account for what we saw, what we smelled, what we touched, and where it went. Al was convinced the money was counterfeit, and the more he looked at it and thought about it, the more convinced he became. "This is how they get it into circulation," he said, "It all gets pumped out through legitimate transactions until the fake stuff becomes real." He had to go on to explain how it worked, but I wasn't convinced about any of it. The bundle of tens I was packing into empty potato chip bags looked exactly like the one in my pocket. "If it's that good, it doesn't matter," Al said, which I didn't understand at all. All I knew is that we were stuck inside something we never intended to be a part of. I also knew that we weren't mad about it anymore; we were starting to make some money.

It was an ugly, low-tech operation and Al had a hundred different ideas on how to do it better, but we kept it to ourselves. "That's how we move up," I told him, "but we have to find the right guy to talk to." We hated the job, but after a while we started not minding it, knowing that we wouldn't be doing it forever. We were earners, and by the time we graduated from high school we were making enough money that it didn't seem to make sense to go to college. Al took some vo-tech classes and I took some business classes at the junior college, but mostly we concentrated on work and how to make more money. When we complained that we were still doing the same jobs we'd been doing for almost two years, Potato Chip Guy told us he'd been doing the same job for five times that long. But he was an idiot, so we waited for the right time and finally went to the guy behind the desk and talked to him.

"That's up to you," he told us. "If you see a different job for yourself, let me know what it is. If it doesn't exist, we'll see if we can't create it for you. But if there's someone already doing it, you'll stay where you are until a position opens up."

"He's talking about us creating a vacancy," Al said later. "That's how it works."

"How?"

"He's talking about us getting rid of someone."

"No, he's not."

"Yes, he is. That's how it's always done. The lower guys take out somebody and move on up."

"Maybe that's how it used to be done, but not anymore. Except in the movies."

"That's how it's done every day. Look at the cartels in Mexico, look anywhere."

"I'm not doing it," I said. "I couldn't. Could you?"

"I don't know."

"What we're doing is petty," I said. "If we get caught it's nothing, probably not even jail time. If we knock some guy off, that's an entirely different thing. Besides, what you're talking about makes no sense."

"What does make sense?"

"We buy the guy out. You pay him enough to not work and he'll let us take over."

"America likes winners and losers, and nothing in between. You can't win unless someone else loses. That's what it's like. Capitalism and violence are our two greatest inventions. And you can't have one without the other."

"Maybe we'll find another way that works," I said. "Can't we at least try?"

We never got the chance. Potato Chip Guy dropped dead of a heart attack a few days later. Hit the floor right after breakfast.

I tried to keep an eye on Al while I drove into the city, but he didn't show anything, just sat there staring straight ahead. I let him think about it for a while, if he was thinking at all. We were coming up on the beginnings of urban sprawl at the outskirts of the city, self-storage facilities, big -box stores, strip malls, and shopping plazas. There were long lines at the drive-thrus as people waited in a hurry to get breakfast. I had to pay attention to the increasing number of morons on the road and forget about my passenger for a minute. We were still a good twenty minutes from where we needed to be. I glanced over; Al hadn't moved, maybe hadn't even blinked.

"You know the story you're going to tell?" I said.

Al stared straight ahead as if I hadn't said anything.

"I've got it covered," I told him.

"What are you going to say?"

"Don't worry about it. Let's worry about what else is going on."

"What do you mean?"

"You tell me. First your hard drive and now this. What's going on?"

"I don't know. Somebody's after me, I guess."

"No. They're after us. If they're coming for you, they're coming for the both of us."

"I don't know," Al said. "What are you going to say when we get in there?"

"Don't worry about it."

We pulled into the parking garage and I drove past a number of empty spots until I saw what I was looking for. Sara was parked away from everybody, my old Honda sitting there, waiting. I pulled in next to her and went to the Honda and got two metal suitcases out of the back. I went to the driver's door and she lowered the window. "Don't take any detours on the way back. Go on to school."

"Yes, Dad," she said.

"Thanks. I'll see you later."

Al and I watched her leave and I handed a case to him and we went inside.

"How'd you know?"

"I didn't," I said. "But it seemed like a good time to start doing things different. Don't say anything when we go in there. But look. Look at them and see if you notice anything when we walk in. You know what I mean?"

"I know."

"Let me do the talking. You just keep your eyes on them."

We took the elevator up to the thirty-first floor—just like in that song by the Flying Burrito Brothers—and Al and I both held on tight to our cases even though no one was taking the ride with us. We stopped at the reception desk and announced our presence, and the guy sitting there who'd seen us enter around the same time for the past ten or twelve Fridays had to pick up the phone like he did every Friday and check and then tell us to go on in. I don't know how many receptionists we've seen, but they all do it the same way, exactly the same way.

We walked into the room and [redacted] was standing next to his desk when we came in. There was another man in the room, also standing, as if they were just finishing up a meeting and exchanging goodbyes. [redacted] and the man looked at us as if we barely warranted attention, like a couple of waiters bringing breakfast. let us stand there a second longer than comfortable. There was no surprise in his face, no disappointment, nothing to register that he knew anything about what had happened on the road. He just stood there and looked at us the same way he did every Friday and then motioned us toward the desk. He didn't introduce the other man and the man didn't leave, or didn't hurry in leaving, I should say. He lingered longer than I would have liked, as if waiting for something to be said or done, so we all stood around awkwardly, with Al and I holding our cases, and standing near his desk looking at us and us looking at him, and the man finally left, wordlessly and anonymously. I'd never seen him before, and Al said he didn't know who he was. I wondered if he was there just to see us enter the room, just to see if we'd come empty-handed or not. When you don't know the whole story, you start to think that everyone is part of the plot. Sometimes, however, they're just extras, people who have nothing at all to do with your story. Sometimes.

Al and I put the cases next to 's desk and I decided to tell him what had happened.

"Where'd you get pulled over?"

"About five miles out of Berling," I said.

"And you didn't know the cops? Never seen them before?"

"Never," I said.

"But you think they knew you?"

"They seemed to know where to look," I said. "And they had no cause to pull us over."

"But they had cause to search."

"That's my fault," I said. "I'd forgotten about a bottle in the back. That was probable cause, they said."

"Local or state cops?"

"Local."

"Describe them."

Al and I were in agreement on the first one, the one that approached us and searched the car. We disagreed on the other one. Al even contradicted me on him.

"He was taller than me," I said. "Taller than six feet."

"No," Al said. "He wasn't. People look taller in those situations."

I shook my head. "He was standing right there next to me," I said. "I know he was taller. And I think he had a tattoo on his right hand, I saw some ink peeking out from his sleeve."

"I didn't see it," Al said and I shot him a look.

"I saw it. I couldn't make out any design, but there was ink there."

We weren't helping and ████████ grew tired of us and changed the subject.

"So they searched the car and didn't find anything. Why is that?"

"Something told me to switch it up this week," I said. "I've never liked this part of the arrangement. You know that. I'm always worried something might happen on the way. Plenty of pirates in the sea, you know."

████████ ignored me. As far as he was concerned, getting him his money every Friday was the only thing I had to do in my life and he didn't really care about how it happened or what problems I had along the way. He cared about cops, though, and cared if they acted like they knew something, or seemed to know something (both of which are rarities). He took our cases and counted his money and placed it in a box on his side of the desk.

"Not a bad week," he said, "a little lighter than usual."

"Could have been a lot lighter," Al said.

"What do you want to do about next week?" I said.

"Any ideas?"

"You could get us an armored truck," Al said, "something official looking. Maybe a cop car of our own."

████ laughed, dismissing the whole thing.

"Next week will be different," he said, as if he could see that far into the future. Maybe he could. All I could see was more of the same, and not much of it good. From where we stood, anyway. From the other side of the desk it all probably looked just fine.

"We should think of something, just in case," I said.

"Maybe you should," he said, putting it all back on me.

We took our empty cases and went back to the car. We didn't stop for breakfast, we didn't do anything in the city. We just got back in the car and headed for home, and I started thinking about what to do about next week. Next week, it turned out, was never going to happen. I should have been thinking about what to do about tomorrow.

"What did you think of that?" I asked Al on the way home.

"I didn't like that guy being there."

"You think he was there for us?"

"No," Al said. "I just didn't like him."

"How'd ████ seem to you?"

"Same as always. You don't think he's the one who sent the cops? He wouldn't steal his own money."

"Stranger things have happened," I said. "Besides, it may be his money about as much as it is ours. We don't really know." We didn't. We'd been bringing the laundry to ████ for years, but for all we knew he had to turn around and hand it over to someone else. We didn't know the operation and we didn't know how it all worked. All we had to know was our part of it.

"I don't think he'd use cops," Al said.

"Maybe they weren't cops," I said. I had no idea what I was talking about.

"We could check it out," Al said. "Go back and watch the station."

"And then what?"

"I don't know."

"Me you want to kill. These guys today, who definitely wanted to rob us, you don't know."

"I thought you stole my money. These guys weren't taking my money. Or setting my house on fire."

At least we could joke about it. A little.

"You think it's the same guys?"

"I don't know."

"Me neither," I said. "I guarantee they're not done with us, though."

Al wasn't so sure. He grabbed the bottle from the back seat and poured some into his mug. If it had been a few years ago, before his wife died, I wouldn't be worried. That Al could take care of himself, take care of his wife, and me and Sara. A little drink in him seemed to sharpen him, not dull him the way it did now. He had always been the one in charge, ever since we were kids, but now he followed. After his wife died, he gave up. You couldn't blame him. It had been a fight, a fucking all-out brawl that they both fought with everything they had and still lost, and Al was beaten down and for a while we weren't sure he was going to get back up. The fact that he could do anything, walk out the door and face the world, let alone get back into business, especially the business we did, was a miracle. He'd carried me for a long time, the least I could do was carry him for a while. But Al was the brains and the muscle; I did whatever he told me and after a while he didn't have to tell me anymore. I knew what he wanted me to do and didn't have to think about it, the way Zeno knows what's expected of him, the way he anticipates what I want him to do. I wasn't sure I could be on the other end of the leash, the one needing to take control when necessary. It had been easy; Al had made it easy and anything is easy when it's running smooth. The test comes when it doesn't. Al wasn't completely out of his head mad at me, but we weren't back to where we were before, either. He didn't entirely trust me right now and I didn't trust him, either. I can recall that when he finished pouring the liquor into his mug, he put the whiskey bottle on the back seat. Did he always do that, or did he put it there for the cops? I seem to remember that he always put it under his seat. I can see him do it. Did he always do it that way? Maybe he did, and maybe he didn't today to give the cops probable cause. "He wouldn't steal his own money," Al said, but maybe he would, maybe if he was going to get more back than he had before. You can play it a lot of ways, especially when you don't know the truth. Instead, you just go round and round with doubts and possibilities and suspicions. I looked over at him and tried to figure out what he was thinking. I used to know, or thought I knew. I wondered about the bottle. Did he ever put it in the back seat before? Maybe he did all the time. To be honest, I couldn't remember. I'm not usually paying attention to stuff like that. I'm driving. Besides, it's Al's car; he can put stuff wherever he wants. The problem is, I never questioned my trust in him, and now it was gone. That's a worse loss than a hard drive or money, much worse. Especially in our line of work. I needed someone to trust, absolutely, and someone I could confide in, talk things through, to test how stupid I was and try to get smarter in a hurry. That someone was going to be Sara..

When we took over the business, expectations were high that we'd do better than our predecessor. "You wanted it," told us. "Now let's see what you can do with it." To be honest I didn't know what to do. The Flying F was now in my name and I wanted to be careful with how much money came through it.

"We can't give them what they've been getting," Al said. "That's not going to make anyone happy." Stating the obvious was not going to help either.

The only thing I could think of was to capitalize on our names. At least on paper, Al and I were strangers, so I thought we could create a number of separate entities that did business together. I had no idea what that would be, however.

Al started looking into opportunities around town. He bought the hardware store and lumberyard, and when the subdivision started, he created LLCs to purchase our houses as well as the undeveloped lots. Then he really went to work. He started working with wire transfers, traveler's checks, and foreign exchanges, especially *casas de cambio* deals. He was moving small amounts, but lots of them, then he started targeting banks that needed deposits, providing fake paperwork or sometimes no paperwork, especially Mexican banks. He used his father's name, or a variation of it. Within a couple of years, Al had doubled the amount of money we were moving. He even bought property in Mexico with his father's name. "Maybe it means something to them," he said. He wanted me to buy the lot next to him. "I'm not going to Mexico," I said.

"You never know," I remember he said.

"We live in the golden age of fraud," a hedge fund manager from the city told me one night over drinks at the Flying F, back when I still owned it and worked behind the bar every once in a while. He was bragging about how much money he made and how little he paid in taxes—all drunkenly out of the blue, by the way—and started to tell me about his own methods of taking money that wasn't his and hiding it from the government or whoever. He'd had enough to drink. I poured him another.

"You shouldn't tell me your inside game," I told him. "Maybe I work for the IRS and moonlight as a bartender."

He waved my objection away with a small flick of his wrist. "That's the thing," he said. "Knowing how to do it is one thing, but actually doing it is something else. You have to be inside to play the game. You can't do it standing behind a bar."

"I won't be standing here forever," I said, but he'd stopped listening. If he ever did. When the time came, I added a few more charges to his credit card. I could make more than enough money standing exactly where I was.

Everything was going so well that when the pandemic and lockdown hit, we were hardly affected at all. The bar was closed, but we were running takeout food out of the restaurant. Three meals seven days a week, and most people were paying cash. And people still needed stuff from the hardware store, and the price of lumber went through the roof. And then there was crypto. Al had introduced it to our boss early on, and over the years showed [illegible] how it worked and how it could make him more money. He was like a prospector selling maps, picks, and shovels. Except there was actual gold where he promised. He made a lot of money for our boss and whoever his boss is and so on. And he made some money for himself, stuck on the missing hard drive.

Sara knows people. She knows them a lot better than I do, and more of them. She pays attention, and actually likes other people. The number of people I like can be counted on one hand, even with a couple of fingers cut off. I've grown up in this town, been here my whole life, and don't really know anybody. I know all about them, don't get me wrong, know who can be trusted and who can't be trusted. I've even employed a good number of the townspeople, as waitstaff, cooks, dishwashers, bartenders, accountants, lawyers, contractors, plumbers, electricians, mechanics, and I still don't know them, not really. When I was more involved with the bar I knew them better, but even then it was more my wife. She was the face of the operation. She liked people too. Too much, it turns out. Anyway, when I ran the bar I saw everybody come through and I was always friendly, knew the regulars, kept my eyes and ears open, but it was all surface, no real friendships. Nobody to have anything to do with outside of the bar. I didn't need anyone else. I had my wife, my daughter, and my brother. If you have three people in your life who you can confide in, can count on, and can accept for who they are and who accept you for who you are, totally and completely, that's all you need. The problems come when that number gets subtracted. I couldn't trust my wife, it turns out, and now I'm not sure about my brother. We'll see if one is enough. The prospects of addition don't look too good.

The only person who comes close is Fitz. He's run the bar for almost five years, and I trust him. Or I should say I trust him with his business; I don't trust him with mine. I sold him the bar after my divorce, in a moment of rash decisions. I thought maybe I'd get out of town, get away from the talk and the rumors and all that. But Sara wanted to stay with me, and she wanted to stay in town with her school and her friends. Maybe when she goes to college I'll leave. If I even make it that far. Anyway, Fitz owns the bar, but the business runs like usual. I still help him with the books, and Fitz is about as interesting as a blank page. He is genial, has a nice broad, friendly smile with straight white teeth, and people seem to go for that sort of thing, but he is as shallow as an empty teaspoon and I've never heard him say one interesting sentence about anything other than business all the years I've known him. He's perfect. People like him and he likes them, and I don't have to deal with any of them. I don't deal with customers, I don't deal with staff, I don't deal with anything I don't want to. I don't even have keys to the place, which I'm only reminded of when I have to bang on the door some Thursday morning and some new kid doesn't know who the hell I am. It's my own fault, I tell myself. Maybe I should go around more often, introduce myself, let them get to know who I am so they can act like they give a shit. But I don't want to, which is why I'm where I am. Fitz is not moving up. There's only me and Sara, and Zeno. Zeno is more interesting and trustworthy and loyal than almost any person I know, and if he could talk and drive a car we'd be all set.

Zeno was fed and I had dinner ready and waiting and texted Sara, "Where are you?"

"On my way home."

I hated that response. It didn't tell me anything, except she knew she was late. She didn't have to eat dinner with me if she didn't want to, as long as she let me know beforehand. That was one of the few rules we had. It was different when she was younger and I ran the bar and other stuff and no one knew where I was most of the time, including myself. I'd get home early in the morning and sleep until the afternoon and maybe see Sara for a little while before I had to go back and do it all over again. Sometimes I wouldn't see her for days.

"You're going to regret it," Al told me. "You're going to miss her whole childhood and then she'll be out of the house and you'll regret it."

He was right, and I started to change, to make sure I was around after school, taking her to piano lessons and horse riding and tennis, trying to play tennis with her, trying to do whatever she wanted, being there for her whenever she needed me. It paid off when it counted the most. When her mom wanted to leave, she left, but she also left Sara, and at least Sara still had me. We had each other. Most things in life don't work out; at least that did. So far, anyway.

She came through the kitchen door about half an hour later with a half-hearted "sorry" and an appetite.

"Where were you?"

"Kelly's," she said and that was the entire explanation. It didn't matter. I wanted to do the explaining. She sat and listened as I went through and told her what had happened. I wasn't expecting her to figure things out for me, but I thought that if I went through it again, maybe I could figure it out. It turns out that Sara knew more than I did.

"You know anybody over in Berling?" I asked her.

She shook her head. "They knew what they were looking for, though, right?"

"Seemed that way."

"And what about the bottle?"

"I don't know," I said. "I honestly don't know. Why would Al tip them?"

"What if he's in a situation where he has to?" Sara said.

"What do you mean?"

"I'm not meaning anything. I'm just saying, what if he's in a tough spot and didn't know what else to do? What if he did it because he had to, you know?"

"Then he's in a worse spot than he was this morning. Should I talk to him?"

"You can't talk to him, not about this. He can't know that you're even thinking about it."

"How am I going to help him?"

"We need to find out who's got him," Sara said.

"There's no 'we' here. I'll find out. I was just talking things out. I'll figure it out."

"I can help with Berling," Sara said.

"How?"

"I'll try. I'll meet some people."

"No, you won't."

"Don't worry, Dad. I won't get any closer to Berling than I am right now."

"I know what that means. It means I'm going to worry."

"Don't. There's nothing to worry about, believe me. Now, what do we know so far? We know the cops were from Berling. We think they knew what they were looking for. And we think Uncle Al might have tipped them off. That's what we know."

"You forgot one thing," I said.

"I don't think so."

"You forget the biggest question of all," I said. "Who took Al's hard drive."

"I didn't forget," Sara said. "I know who took it."

"You do? Who?"

"Me."

"How long do you think we have, in this line of work, I mean?" Al said to me.

"As long as we want. As far as anyone is concerned, we run legitimate businesses. Who can prove otherwise?"

"We could get pushed out, the way we were going to do with Mr. Potato Chip. The way everyone does it."

"Not as long as we keep producing. We'll be fine, Al. Don't worry."

"I'm not worried. But I don't want to end up dead on the floor of some dreary house with coffee waiting on the counter and a van of chips in the drive."

"That's not how it's going to happen. You'd never own a van."

"I'm planning ahead," Al said. "I'm not going to prison."

"You're not going to," I told him. "We're smarter than that."

"Someone could turn on us."

"Not if we turn on them first."

"You'd do that?"

"No," I said. "I don't know. Depends on what the situation is. If it's between you and some other guy, I'm turning."

"That's what I'm worried about," Al said. "I don't want that. I'm going to get out."

"Not now."

"Not now, but soon. Before I'm forty, forty-five at the latest. I'm going to put away enough money for Vera and me to go to Mexico and disappear, maybe live under my father's name. Put that to use for once."

"You don't speak Spanish."

"We'll learn. We have time."

That's when he handed me the envelope. "That's the access code to my crypto," he said. "Just in case anything happens to me, you can get the money and make sure Vera has it."

"Nothing's going to happen," I said.

"You don't know that. Just keep it. Somewhere safe. I'll sleep better knowing you have it. Do that for me."

That was almost ten years ago. Then the cancer came. And Al stopped caring, and who could blame him. He cares now, though, and I can't go to him and tell him that Sara is the one who took his money. And she says she can't get it back.

I won't say my father was a criminal. And I won't let him give you all the details of his alleged crimes, and I certainly won't let him use the actual names of people he worked with and for, which would only bring more trouble upon him. I won't let him write his confession, especially not a confession to things he didn't do. I will let him tell his story (to a point)—and he can defend his own actions without my help—but I won't let him put himself in jail. My father has never hurt anyone, has never dealt drugs, engaged in sex trafficking, committed violence, or even knowingly injured someone. He owns a bar and restaurant and handles cash for some people. As far as I know, his books are in order. He pays his taxes, has never been audited or even investigated. I'm not saying he's squeaky clean, and I'm not saying he doesn't know some people who maybe he shouldn't know, but he knows a lot of people and if you run a bar you're bound to know some people you shouldn't, people who have troubles and sometimes those troubles become yours. My father hasn't always been on the right side of the law, but that's mostly rumors and talk. I know my dad. He's certainly a better person than most people in town, and no worse than any of them. If he's done anything wrong, it's not much in the scheme of things, more or less like one of his waitstaff who doesn't report all of their tips to the IRS.

I can tell you that we don't have the kind of money some people might assume we have. If we have it, Dad certainly doesn't spend it. When I got my license he gave me his ten-year-old Honda CR-V. It was an ugly maroon with more than two hundred thousand miles on it. Everybody else in class got a brand-new car. He got the new car, another Honda, but gray this time. "Meteorite gray," Dad corrected me. And that's about as lavish as we live. We have a nice house, and I don't want for anything, but most of my friends have better cars than I do, nicer clothes, go on expensive trips, to private schools, summer camps, and the expensive colleges.

"We don't have to worry about college" is all my father has said about it.

"I'm not worried about college," I said. "I'm worried about my car."

"Your car's fine. And if you ever have any trouble, take it to your uncle, he can probably fix it."

It didn't take long to find the cops who had stopped my father and uncle. They left a slimy little trail all over social media. Young guys who could have used some college themselves instead of going right into the police force. Maybe they could have learned the meaning of discretion. I took note of some of their off-duty locations and sent a couple of friends to see if they could find out something about them.

"Don't get into trouble," I told them. "Just flirt and see if they're dumb enough to tell you anything." I told them to be careful. I should have known better. You put a couple of nice high school girls with guys like that on a Saturday night, of course there's going to be trouble. Luckily, they knew what they were doing, in the end.

"Why would you take Al's hard drive?" I asked Sara.

She looked away from me, her eyes drifting down to Zeno curled up next to her chair, and she looked back at me, her eyes steady and true.

"I wanted to try and stop him from doing something stupid," she said.

"And what's that?"

She looked down again, and when her eyes came back toward me this time, she couldn't look straight at me. I knew she wasn't going to lie to me, but I wasn't sure if she was going to tell me anything. She didn't want to, that was certain.

"I don't know if this is a hundred percent true," Sara said, "but there was talk that Uncle Al was going to turn over information to the DA. And that the information was stored on that hard drive."

"Who told you that?"

"I'm not going to say. Just know it's somebody who doesn't want to see you hurt."

If you would have asked me who that could be, I'd say Sara and Al, and that would be about the complete list. Sitting there in the kitchen, I could not come up with another name. So I said, "Zeno?"

At least she laughed. "He probably knows more than all of us put together," Sara said, "but he keeps it to himself."

"I don't know who it is, but I wish you would tell me."

"I will," Sara said, "but not right now."

We left it at that.

"Where's the hard drive now?"

"Over at Kelly's. We were trying to see if we could break into it, see what's on there."

"A lot of money is all I thought was on there," I said. "It makes sense why he was so mad about it, if there's something else. What did you find?"

"We haven't gotten in yet."

"What did you tell Kelly?" I wasn't sure which Kelly she was talking about but thought it was too late for me to ask without being embarrassed, and it didn't really matter right then.

"Nothing. Doesn't know anything about anything other than I want to access an old drive and don't know the password."

"I had the damn password," I blurted out. "I've had it for years."

"You 'had' it? You don't have it now?"

"I just gave it back to Al, to try and prove to him that I didn't take his hard drive. You shouldn't have taken it."

"Dad."

"I mean it. Or you should have told me first. I had the password. We could have done this all different."

"It's too late for that, Dad."

"We have to give it back."

"What?"

"I'll give it back to Al."

"Dad. You can't do that. What if he turns around and hands it over to the DA?"

"If he's going to turn on me, he's going to do it with or without that hard drive," I said. Then I remembered Mexico. Maybe the money on the hard drive was his retirement stash. He could take his crypto and disappear. "Maybe I should talk to him."

"You can't."

"Somebody's got him in a spot," I said. "Maybe I can help him."

"We have to hang on to the drive," Sara said. "He won't do anything without that. In the meantime, let me work on a few things."

I didn't see Al all weekend. It wasn't typical, but it wasn't unusual either. I tried not to read more into it than it was, which is hard to do after someone has threatened to kill you and then you learn they might be setting you up for arrest, or worse.

Zeno and I took a few walks past his house. He didn't show. Maybe he wasn't around. I texted him that I'd help him with repairs to the garage if he wanted, but he didn't respond. Not for a while, anyway. Then he said, "Maybe later. At the hardware store." I drove down to the hardware store. He wasn't there. I drove around town, passing his usual spots, and hoped that Zeno might spot him and let me know. Zeno sat in the passenger seat, sniffing out the partially opened window, and didn't say anything. In the afternoon, I drove to the Flying F and looked at the lunch crowd, the people scattered at tables finishing their lunches, and the regulars at the bar, hunched over their drinks or watching basketball on the TVs. Fitz was wandering around, chatting with the customers, and I took a seat at the bar. The kid from the other day brought me a seltzer with lime—Fitz must have given him a good lesson after we left—and I waited. I glanced up at the screen. March Madness. If they only knew.

Fitz took his time. That's the way you do it, you listen and talk as long as the customer wants. You don't say anything more than they want to hear, and you don't excuse yourself before they're done talking. It's simple. I could never do it. I never had enough to say, and I never wanted to hear most of what they told me. Fitz was cut out for this kind of work. He seemed genuinely interested in people. It showed. I glanced back at the screen, another commercial. It seemed like that's all it was, commercials interrupted every once in a while by college kids wanting to play a game. Everybody's always waiting on someone.

I remember hearing a New York restaurant owner talk about what he learned from more than twenty years in the business. "If you see a regular customer every week for fifty-one weeks and you give him a free drink the fifty-second week, they'll love you; if you give a free drink to the same customer for fifty-one weeks and forget the fifty-second week, they'll hate you." I was almost done with my drink and the kid was nowhere to be seen. I didn't want another one, but I thought about saying something to Fitz. By the time he came over, I'd forgotten about it, or decided not to mention it.

"Sorry about that," Fitz said.

"No need," I said. "I'm the one interrupting." I left the barstool and we went over to a quiet table.

"Off to a good start today, anyway," Fitz said. He saw I didn't have a drink and looked for the kid.

"I'm good," I said. "I had something at the bar."

"I'm getting something. You sure you don't want anything?"

"I'm good," I said.

The kid brought over a couple of seltzers to the table and set them down and left.

"You got his attention," I said.

"A work in progress, but he'll be all right. You'll see."

"You'll see before I do. I know that. You seen Al at all today?"

Fitz shook his head. "I figured maybe for lunch, but it didn't happen. He's not the regular he used to be."

"That's probably for the best. If he comes in, though, let me know."

"You haven't seen him."

"Not since yesterday."

"You think he's back to old habits?"

"No. He's good. Under control, as far as I know."

"And as far as I know. I heard he was doing some day drinking elsewhere, though."

That was news to me. "Where's that?"

"Bishop's Corner."

"Over in Addison?"

"That's what I heard."

"Recently."

"Couple months ago, anyway. I didn't mean to spill something I shouldn't have."

"No. You should have. I appreciate it."

"Least he could do is spend my own money here," Fitz said, trying to make a joke of it. It wasn't like him to say the wrong thing. And maybe it wasn't wrong; it was sort of funny, but I wasn't in the mood.

"It's not your money."

"I didn't mean anything by it."

"We got called out for being light on Friday," I said. "That's on you."

"We'll make up for it this week," Fitz said. "You know how it works."

"I know how it's supposed to work," I said and got up from the table.

Fitz looked for the kid again. "Zeno in the car? I've got something for him." The kid came back with a bag of chicken necks and livers and handed me a couple of napkins. Zeno loves that stuff. I walked out to the car and he knew I had treats; he sat up straight in the passenger seat and started to pant with excitement. I handed him a neck, slightly slick with slime, and he gave it a couple of crunches with his teeth before it was gone. I took a napkin and wiped my hands.

I texted Al again. “Dropped by hardware store. Let me know if you want help/company.”

“Running some errands. Be home later.”

That’s almost as helpful as “on my way home.” Zeno and I drove out to Addison, which was more than thirty minutes away. I tried to tell myself that I knew Al wasn’t going to be there, but if I was so certain why was I driving there? Zeno sat and looked at the bag on the floor and then looked back at me and then back to the bag. “Later,” I told him, and he looked out the window, disappointed.

I pulled into the parking lot of Bishop’s Corner but didn’t see Al’s car. I went inside anyway. They were doing a better business than the Flying F, that’s for sure. I went to the bar and ordered a beer. There were four TVs over the bar, all with commercials on. “Do they ever play basketball,” I said to the bartender when he brought me the beer. He didn’t know what the hell I was talking about.

I took my beer and wandered around, looking for Al. Every guy in the place looked like a cop, I’m not kidding. I figured it was my paranoia. I thought maybe they’d all start looking like the guys from Berling if I stayed there too much longer. They weren’t cops and my brother wasn’t there. After about fifteen minutes I put my full beer down and started to leave when I saw someone I recognized. He didn’t see me and I watched him move through the tables and make his way to the bar. I watched him order a drink and then I approached him. It was the man from Friday, the man we didn’t know standing inside [illegible]’s office. Or at least I didn’t know. I recognized him now. I knew who he was. The Bishops had owned the place for a hundred years or so, and this guy was definitely one of them.

He was drinking a seltzer with lime, which didn’t make me happy. It made me think that maybe he saw me after all. The bartender came over and said, "What can I get you," and I cocked my thumb at the seltzer with lime and told him, "The same."

I turned to the man and said, "Remember me?"

"I know who you are," he said. "What brings you around here?"

"I was hoping to watch the games, but I see you don't have them on."

He looked up the screens and furrowed his brow and decided not to pursue it. It didn't matter, the joke wasn't for him.

"You want something to eat," the man said. "I could get you something."

"That's all right," I said. "I think I've had enough."

"Well, come back any time."

"The next time I come back I'll own the place," I said.

"What makes you think it's for sale?"

"Everything's for sale. Isn't that what you told Fitz?"

"It was just an ask," he said. "If you wanted it, you should have kept it."

"Who says I want it?" I finished my seltzer and went to the car, thinking that if nothing else I knew more than I went in. I'd only suspected that he'd talked to Fitz about buying the bar. Now I knew. I went back to the car. Zeno was lying down on the front seat, his face close to the bag on the floor, but he didn't take anything. He was good; that's one thing I could count on.

"Now who's MIA," Al texted. "Stopped by your house. You're not there."

It made me wonder if someone at Bishop's Corner had tipped him off. That's how you think when you can't trust someone; you think everyone's a cop, or that everyone's in on the conspiracy. I wanted to call Al and have it out in the open right then; I wanted to drive to his house and not leave until we had it all sorted out. Instead, I texted back, "had some shit to sort through. Out with Zeno now. See you later?"

"Not later. Maybe tomorrow."

When I got home, I forgot about tomorrow. Sara told me that she couldn't get back Al's hard drive, not right away. "Kelly gave it to someone who thinks he can hack into it," she said.

"Let's go get it from him, then. Like, right now."

"I'll get it back, Dad. I'll get it back as soon as I can, but not today."

"Why not?"

"Because Kelly FedExed it to the guy. He's in California."

"You're kidding. You're joking with me or mocking me. You can't be fucking serious." I never swore in front of Sara. The word and my tone hit her like a slap I didn't intend.

She didn't say anything.

"Your guy—whoever the fuck he is—can't even attempt to break into that drive. He can't do anything except FedEx it right back. To you. You understand?" Another slap, and a part of me knew that I was raising my voice and adding unintended injury, but the larger part of me, the part that was red -hot, won out.

"I know, Dad."

"What the fuck was Kelly thinking?"

"She was just trying to help. She didn't know."

That was all I got out of it, a pronoun. Otherwise, I was still stuck in some tragic farce, something malicious and straining credulity like the Marquis de Sade directing a play cast with inmates in an asylum. I would have laughed, but Sara was crying.

"Don't cry over it," I said. "But we have to get that back."

"I know," she said, but she didn't stop crying.

Sundays were always family day. Not that Al and I didn't see each other every other day, but it was the day the wives were included, and Sara. Mostly it happened at our house. The wives would cook and Al and I would watch TV or he'd help me with some task, changing the blades on the mower, getting the snow blower to work again, usually something mechanical that I didn't have a clue about. Or we'd play with Sara, sit on the floor and help her build something, destroy something, or let her chase us around, which was a favorite activity from the minute she learned how to run. She loved to chase after Al, would do it all day long if she didn't tire him out. That gave way to baseball and basketball, which Al and I tried to teach Sara until she got better at it than we were, then homework, then, as she approached the land of teen, she wanted less to do with us. Sundays were still for family, however, and she sulked her way through it.

After Vera died, we still carried on, and even after my wife left. But some Sundays—too many to count—Al was in no shape to be around Sara, or anyone for that matter. His Saturday nights had carried over into Sunday mornings, and then Sunday afternoons, and he had to sleep it off to be in shape for Monday. He never missed work and it was a short phase and then was over. I hoped.

Anyway, this Sunday, I didn't want to see him. I didn't want to see him because I didn't know if I could keep my mouth shut. The day before, no problem, but not today, not after the nonsense with the hard drive and chasing him around all day Saturday like a shadow. So I figured I'd better not see him at all. But I spent the whole morning thinking about him, wondering what I would say when I saw him, what I would do, and what I could do to help. I tried to think that he was in trouble and not me. The fact of the matter was, the both of us were in trouble.

By noon, I'd driven myself half crazy, consumed with a storm of thoughts swirling in my head. I couldn't sit around the house and do nothing and I wasn't going to contort myself in knots trying to avoid Al. I drove up to his house. He was in the garage, starting to deal with the charred corner. He was kneeling, scraping around the burned wall, more examining than repairing at this point.

"You need any help?" I said.

He didn't even look at me but continued with his prognosis. "You'd probably set the whole thing on fire. Again."

I didn't know if it was a joke or not, so I ignored it.

"I think I know where your hard drive is," I said. "You want to go get it?"

Al stood up and walked over to me.

"Of course you know where it is."

"Sara found it," I told him. "Or thinks she did."

"Good girl. Let's go get it, then."

"It's on its way to California," I told him.

"What the fuck. What the fuck are you doing to me?"

"I'm trying to help. You want to go to San Francisco? You want to go get it? I'll fly out right now and get the goddam thing. You want to do that?"

"Who's waiting for it in San Francisco?"

"I don't know, Al. But I can find out who it is. We can get there before he even sees it."

"Give me his name, I'll go."

"If you go, I'm going too," I said. The last thing I wanted to do was fly all the way to California, but I wasn't going to let Al go alone—for his sake, my sake, and the well-being of the guy on the other end. Al might have only threatened me, but he would actually kill someone else for it. "I'll take a look at flights." I spent a few minutes on my phone and wondered if I should tell him it wasn't really San Francisco. I decided against it, for now. "There's a four-forty, gets in around eleven-thirty."

"Let's go," Al said.

I went home and called Sara and told her Al and I were going.

"That can't be a good idea," she said.

"We've already booked the flights. I need the address of the guy."

"I don't have it. He's going to ship it right back, Dad. Just give it a couple of days."

"I can't do that. We're going out there."

"You don't even know where you're going. What if I don't get the address?"

"Then you'll have to call your uncle and explain how you're not going to tell him where his property is, the property you stole from him."

"You didn't tell him."

"I didn't tell him that you took it, no. I told him that you found it. He doesn't know any more than that. Give me the address. We're going to go. We are going. You need to take care of Zeno for a couple of days, okay? We should be back Tuesday morning probably, if everything goes the way it should. You'll take care of Z-man?"

"Yes."

"You need to take him for a walk tomorrow and Tuesday morning, come back around noon and let him out for a bit, and make sure he gets fed and spend some time with him, you know."

"I know. I really don't think you should be going, Dad."

"Don't worry. I'll make sure Al doesn't do anything to the guy."

"I'm not worried about that. I'm worried about you and Al."

"We'll be all right. Just get me the address."

"Okay."

"I love you. And don't forget about Zeno."

"I know. I love you too."

I threw a few things in a backpack and Al came and picked me up and we drove to the airport. I don't think we said more than ten words to each other, and none of them were of any importance, none of them meant anything.

We checked in at the airport and I noticed that Al had booked us in different rows, him close to the front and me in the back, in a middle seat.

"Thanks for that," I said. "It's okay if you didn't want to sit with me, but did you have to put me back in the shitter?"

"I got what was available," he said. "If you want to sit in the front, go ahead."

I let him sit in front. I stuffed myself into the middle seat and decided not to fight for my rightful share of the armrests. I texted Sara that we were about to take off. "Maybe I'll know where we're going before we land," I added. The guy next to me tried to read my text and I shot him a look that should have stung for a few time zones. I switched the phone to airplane mode and put it away. I'd brought along a couple of books that Sara had given me, *The Man in the High Castle* and *McTeague*. I figured they were books she had to read for school, but she said no, they were stuff she and Kelly picked out. "Why these?" I said.

"You'll have to figure that out when you read them," Sara said.

I opened *McTeague* and tried to read, but couldn't get past the first page and switched to the other one. I'd read each line and get to the bottom of the page and have no idea what I'd just read and start over and end up where I'd been before. I couldn't concentrate. So I sat there staring at the open book and tried to ignore the people to my right and left.

The last time Al and I had been on a plane was before Sara was born. The four of us—Al and me and our wives—had gone to Cancun for vacation. The whole thing was a disaster, from the minute we arrived to the minute we left. Workers had walked off the job—on strike or just plain quit, it was never entirely clear—and there was a long wait at the airport for cars to our resort, and once we got there, there was hardly any service. We had to wait hours for our bags to get to the room.

"We should have just carried them ourselves," Al kept saying, but when I suggested we walk back and get them, he didn't want to go. "Watch," he said, "when we go, they'll be on their way here." We couldn't even go to the beach because we were still in street clothes from the plane. We went to the bar, where there was one bartender and a room full of people who had the same troubles we had and the same idea.

"If you want dinner, you should order it now," another guest told us. It wasn't even three in the afternoon.

She was right. The restaurants were understaffed, in the kitchen, in the front of the house, everywhere. And there was nowhere to go. You couldn't get a car to leave the resort. We were trapped. They didn't even come to clean the room the next day. Al couldn't take it. He was ready to get on the next flight to anywhere. "You're on vacation," Vera told him, "just relax. We've got nothing but time."

Al was particularly annoyed that people spoke Spanish to him and called him Alejandro or by his last name, and he was embarrassed every time he had to say "no hablo" and the fact that I could communicate better than he could. I didn't know much, but you can't work in a restaurant without learning a thing or two.

We tried to make the best of it, spending as much time away from the room, the restaurants, and the bars as possible. We went to the beach, or went golfing. Even that was a shit show. We came back from completing the third hole to find our clubs had been stolen right off the cart. We stood there for a few minutes, completely dumbfounded, when a couple of kids came out of nowhere, carrying our bags.

"We found these over there," they said, pointing to some imaginary spot in the distance. They wanted fifty bucks for each bag. We gave them forty dollars for the four of them.

Al actually enjoyed it. "That's a nice racket," he said. "They take our clubs, then sell them back to us."

"I bet they would have taken twenty for them," Vera said.

Al shrugged. "Maybe it's enough that they won't take someone else's."

"Or you just set the going rate," Vera said.

"Next time I won't give them anything," Al said.

By the fourth day, even Vera was sick of the place. There was no food at breakfast, we'd wait for hours for lunch, and the restaurant was always packed with the same people with the same complaints. We left three days early and headed back home.

"Well, that was fun, where to next time?" Al joked when we landed back home. But there wasn't a next time.

I'm getting sentimental in my old age. You know you're in trouble when you start thinking about the shitty times with fondness. It was a horrible trip. We shouldn't have laughed about it, we shouldn't have tolerated it. Al was right, we should have left immediately and gotten all of our money back. He still likes to tell his golf story, though. Otherwise, leave the past where it belongs. There are better days ahead. You have to believe that. What's the alternative?

Luckily I dozed off before I could get too nostalgic and when I woke up we were in our final descent. As soon as we landed, I checked my phone. Sara had sent the address and I put it into the GPS app. We were about twenty minutes away from the airport. Then I remembered. It's not like we could drive right over and get Al's hard drive. We were there before the package. There was a hotel about ten minutes away. I bookmarked it and waited to get the hell off the plane.

Al was waiting in the terminal and we walked down to the rental car counters.

"I got the address," I told him. "And a hotel."

"I thought we'd drive right over to the spot," Al said.

"We don't have to sleep in the car, you know," I said. "FedEx isn't going to come in the middle of the night."

"I don't want to miss it," he said. A couple more seconds and he'd be entrenched and unmovable.

"Look," I said. "We'll get a room, and if you want to go over to the spot, go ahead and go. I'll sleep a couple of hours and then come and spell you, and you can go back to the room."

"Okay," he said, not thrilled by the idea. Al could always be cheap, that was his default, even if he had a couple of million on a hard drive showing up in a few hours.

I booked the room and texted Sara while he waited in line for the car.

We checked into the hotel and the woman at the counter began going on about all of the attractions nearby, the Paramount Theatre and Lakeside Park and the Cathedral of Christ the Light or some shit like that, and she didn't notice the look on Al's face. I thought he was going to choke her or stuff his bag down her throat.

"We just need the key," he said, talking over me.

"It's late," I said, "and we've had a long flight and an early morning coming."

We got up to the room and I washed the miles off my face and brushed my teeth and by the time I was done, Al was asleep on one of the beds. I set an alarm for five and turned on the TV with the volume too low to hear and stared at the picture for a while, waiting for Al to wake up. I wanted to go over everything one more time, to get on the same page with him. I sat and watched the images flash on the screen and listened to the low hum of the air conditioner and lasted about five minutes before I was out for the night.

We grabbed some breakfast in the hotel and drove over to the address Sara had given me. I'd put the tracking number into the app and it showed an afternoon delivery so I said we should find something else to do for a few hours, but Al didn't want to hear it. He wanted to wait. For as long as it took.

"They're never right with that stuff," he said, and I couldn't argue with that. They tell you it's going to arrive one day and it always comes the next. That's what usually happens, but I wasn't going to tell him that. I didn't want to spend another day sitting in a car almost three thousand miles from where I wanted to be. I didn't want to waste any more time than absolutely necessary.

The place was a three-story concrete box with four balconies on the front and a three-car garage below. I walked up to the mailboxes and confirmed the name Sara had given me. *M. Rutkowska. #3.* I walked up to the door, just to locate it, and made sure Al could see me from the street. I walked back down and returned to the car.

"Who is this guy, anyway?" Al said.

"I don't know. A friend of a friend of Sara's. Somebody sent him the drive by mistake."

"Mistake?"

"They didn't know it was yours," I said. "He doesn't know what it is. Somebody just wanted to get into it and see what was on it."

"They can't get in."

"I know, Al. Like I said, it was a mistake. Just some people hoping to hack something they got by mistake. That's what's going on. Sara found out about it and figured out it was your hard drive."

"How did she know that?"

"I don't know, Al. She knows a lot of people. She's connected. She thinks it must be yours."

"Thinks? You mean she's not sure?"

"She's pretty sure. I mean, she's not the one who sent it out here, but she's pretty sure it's yours. Don't get all worked up about it yet. Let's wait and see."

"What else does Sara know about it?"

"Nothing," I said.

"She doesn't know what's on it?"

"I don't even know what's on it," I said. "Except for the crypto. And I don't even know how much of that."

He didn't say anything.

"Al, we wouldn't do anything to hurt you. You know that. We love you. Sara loves you and I love you."

He didn't say anything. He kept his eyes on the building across the street, an ugly concrete block with twelve windows, six on one side, then the entryway, and six over the row of garage doors—four the same size as the ones on the other side with two smaller ones stacked, probably in a stairway. I tried not to look at it all the time—I knew nothing was going to happen for hours, maybe longer than that—but my attention kept turning back to it, it's gray blankness pulling me back, like watching a prison and hoping there's going to be an escape.

It was a little after nine back home and I texted Sara and reminded her to walk Zeno and come and check on him at noon. She texted back a while later with a photo of Zeno at the end of his leash, looking happy that he was with Sara on a walk for a change. I thought about showing Al the picture, but didn't. He was staring at his concrete.

I called Fitz and told him I was on the West Coast. He didn't ask what I was doing and I didn't tell him. "Anyway, you'll have to get to the bank today, and maybe tomorrow," I said. "I might be back earlier, but I'll let you know later. Okay."

Al called his manager of the hardware store and didn't say anything other than he wouldn't be in. He was better with people than I was but not by much, and he could be worse, much worse.

Finally, around eight, a few people started to leave the building. None of them came out of door #3 but Al and I studied the two men who left, wondering if either one of them could possibly be our guy.

It was afternoon and I started looking for someplace to get something to eat.

"Pizza and pizza look like our options," I said, "if you want me to walk."

"Sounds like it's going to be pizza," Al said.

I got out of the car and started walking. I hoped FedEx wouldn't come while I was away, Al could make things ugly in a hurry. I called in an order and it was ready by the time I got to the restaurant. It was about a fifteen-minute walk back to the car. I had a cardboard box of pizza in one hand and a bag of drinks in the other and the thought kept swirling around my head that I would see a FedEx truck up ahead and have to drop everything and run. By the time I made it back to the car, I wish I had seen a truck, anything except the apartment building and my brother sitting there staring at it. No one had come or gone and Al stared and stared, as if the truck might show up at any second.

"Maybe he's not even there," I said. "We can just walk up to the door and take it when it comes."

Al nodded and kept studying.

"How do you want to play this?" I said.

"What do you mean?"

"What's your plan on getting the package?"

"When the driver comes, we take it."

"He's not going to give it to us. He's only going to give it to the person on the package."

"Then we follow him to the door and take it then."

"Let's do this without too much force, okay?"

"I'll use as much force as I need."

"How about this? We let the FedEx guy deliver the package, leave, and then we go and get it from the guy, from Rutkowska. That way, you only have one guy to deal with, instead of possibly two."

"What if he doesn't open the door?"

"He'll open the door. If he doesn't, then you can go nuts. Be my guest."

Al thought about it and must have agreed in his silence.

"Seven million on it," Al said almost out of nowhere.

"Seven?"

"Seven million sitting right there in the desk drawer. Could be more now. I haven't been checking. I don't want to know until I get it back. You heard about that guy who lost his drive in the dump? Accidentally threw out his drive. He had more than a quarter of a billion on it. Can you imagine? At the bottom of a trash heap."

"You have to forget about it at that point, don't you?"

"Try forgetting about a quarter of billion dollars."

"What else did you have on it?"

"What, seven million dollars isn't enough for you, Peck?"

The FedEx guy drove up a little after five and we watched him hit a couple of houses on the opposite side of the street before he went back into the truck and got the only package in the entire world that we were interested in.

Al got out of the car and hurried over to the apartment building while the driver was at the truck. The driver looked tired or disinterested, or both. He didn't look around, his eyes focused on the task at hand, the package in one hand and his device in the other.

He started up the stairs and Al came down. I turned the ignition of the car. I could see Al talking to the guy and the guy shaking his head. Al might be trying to pass himself off as M. Rutkowska. The driver wasn't buying it. Al turned and started following the driver for a few steps before he grabbed the package and yanked it out of the driver's hand. Al sprinted down the steps and into the car. I was pulling away before he had the door closed.

I drove for a few blocks before I was convinced that the driver wasn't going to follow us. "Why would he?" Al said. "He's not going to stick his neck out about it. He'll just submit a report."

"It wasn't how I thought we were going to play it," I said.

"Sometimes direct action is the most effective," Al said, satisfied with himself. He opened the package to make sure it was the drive. It was.

"Where'd you learn that grab-and-go move, anyway?"

"TikTok or some shit like that," Al said, and we both laughed. I drove a few more blocks and then pulled to the curb. I called Sara.

"We've got the drive," I said.

"Put her on speaker," Al said. I ignored him.

"We didn't see the guy," I said. "Al got it from the driver, so make sure that Kelly tells the guy that we got it."

Al grabbed the phone from me and put Sara on speaker.

"Who is this guy, anyway?"

"I don't know," Sara said. "Somebody Kelly knows."

"Who's Kelly?"

"A friend of mine."

"And what's your friend doing with my drive in the first place?"

"I gave it to her, Al. You know that. And you know why I gave it to her."

"I don't know anything," Al said. "And I especially don't know about Kelly."

Al was seething now, his voice close to a yell. Sara, on the other hand, remained calm.

"It's okay," Sara said. "You've got your drive back. Everything's okay."

"Everything's fine," I said. "Just tell Kelly to call the guy."

"I want to talk to Kelly," Al said.

"Maybe when we get back," I said.

"Who's this guy who was going to get my drive?" Al said.

"I don't know," Sara said. "Just some guy."

"Just some guy," Al said. "He's not just some guy. You don't send a drive all the way to California to 'just some guy.' It doesn't make sense."

"He's just a guy Kelly knows. He's good with this kind of stuff. So Kelly thought he could help. That's all I know about it. I gave the drive to Kelly and she sent it off to the guy. He was going to see if he could take a look at the drive. That's all he was doing. And that's all I know about it. Except now you have it and no one's seen it and no one knows what's on it except you, Uncle."

"That's right," I said. "Al's got it. No one's looking at it. You don't need to talk to Kelly," I added to Al as I finished the call with Sara.

"I want to talk to her," Al said, and the conversation escalated again until he was yelling at me. You couldn't talk to Al when he was all worked up like that. He was like a dog in the red zone, gnashing and snarling and not listening. Only Al was practically foaming at the mouth about it. He was a bit too worked up about it, I thought, and I suddenly became suspicious. I thought maybe he was trying to set a trap, trying to get me to tell him something I shouldn't. The trouble is, he had me at a disadvantage. He might know more about it than I did. Sara talked to him about this kind of stuff, personal stuff, a lot more than she did with me. I always liked that part of their relationship. Sara needed that, and so did Al. But now I didn't know what he knew about it. She might have talked to Al about Kelly.

"You know Kelly,"I said, which got him even more worked up.

"I don't know any Kelly. And I certainly didn't know she had my drive. What the fuck are you talking about."

"Take it easy, Al. Calm down and think about it. Kelly's a friend of

Sara's. Maybe you don't know her, but you've heard Sara mention her. They've been spending a lot of time together. You know that. She's not some random person. You know who she is."

He calmed down, but only a little. "I know who you mean," he said, and then I wasn't sure that he did. Maybe now he was bluffing. I couldn't read him. I was too much in my own head about it. Al wasn't being the cagey one; it was me, and to no purpose really, except I was afraid, afraid that the fury he had with me about his drive would be turned on Sara, or Kelly, or both. That was legitimate. Al could cause harm when he wanted, no matter what.

"You can talk to Kelly and Sara when we get home," I said. "But do we have to think about that now? We got what we came for, so can we think about getting the hell out of here as soon as possible and getting home?"

Al booked us on the red-eye, and after the excitement had worn off I started to worry that solving Al's problem was only going to worsen my own, and Al started chewing at the same old bone.

"I still can't figure out why this Kelly person shipped my drive out here?" Al said as we drove to the airport.

"I don't know. All I know is that she and Sara got it back for you. That's who Kelly is. The person who helped you get your stuff back."

"There's more to it than that."

"I don't think there is. But let me ask this," I said. "Let's say for argument's sake that no one knows about the contents of the drive, except you and me. I've never told anyone about it—never—so if anyone else knows, that's on you. Let's keep that in mind. But for a minute, let's say no one knows about the money. Is there anything, anything at all, on that drive that someone would want?"

Al turned and looked me squarely in the eyes and said, "No."

Now I had a choice to make. Either Sara was lying or Al was. Either Sara stole the drive and lied about why she had, or Al was lying about what was on it. They both couldn't be telling the truth, and I had to figure out who I was going to believe. I wasn't good at this. I thought I could trust both of them completely and fully, that they would never knowingly lie to me and deceive me. They never had, as far as I knew, and they never would. But one of them was. Of course, I'd thought that way once before, had complete and total faith in someone, and she lied to me, lied straight to my face with the same look that Al just had. And she broke my heart. Of course she'd lied to Sara too, and Al. She'd hurt all of us, but I was the one who couldn't get over it.

There was the tiniest loophole here, though. Maybe they both were telling the truth. Sara didn't know for sure what was on the drive. She'd only been told that something was on it, that Al was going to hand over information on me. She didn't know what the information was and if it was even really on the drive. Maybe she'd been lied to. She wouldn't tell me who it was. She didn't have to. I knew. I fucking knew.

"Maybe you told Sara about the money," Al said.

"No. No. No."

"Maybe Cheryl, then."

"Shut it down now, Al."

"I'm sorry I brought her up," Al said, "sorry I said the name no one is ever supposed to say, sorry I made mention of her at all. But maybe, just maybe, in the time you were together, you mentioned the envelope. Maybe she asked about it. Maybe you told her by accident. Maybe."

"Absolutely not. I swear to fucking God, Al, I've never told anyone. Because if you want to know the absolute truth, you gave me the envelope and I put it in the safe and that was the last I thought of it. I don't really care what you have on the drive and I never really wanted to be responsible for it anyway, if you remember. But you insisted that I keep your envelope—which you now have, remember—so I kept it. And I kept it secret, like I've kept all your secrets, because you can trust me. I hope you can say the same."

"Let's talk when someone's walked off with seven million dollars of your money."

We checked in for the flight and Al had stuck me in the last row again, while he was up near the front. We had time to kill so we went and got something to eat. We finished eating and still had time to kill. We decided to go to the gate and found plenty of empty seats. About when I started reading, Al decided to start talking again.

"What's with all the saints," he said.

"What?"

"We were in Santa Clara earlier, weren't we?"

"Yeah."

"San Francisco, San Diego, San Gabriel, San José, San Luis Obispo, Santa Barbara, Santa Clara, Santa Cruz, everything out here is named after a saint."

"Oakland," I said.

"You want to argue about it? Let me give you some more." He started naming off more cities.

"You're right. But don't blame me. That's your family's doing."

"What do you mean?"

"California was settled by the Spanish. They're the ones with the saint fixation. Blame them."

"You said my family. That's not my family."

"Your dad's, then."

"He's not Spanish."

"You go back far enough, I bet you wind up in Spain. You don't know?"

"I don't care."

"You know where Mom's from?"

"Everywhere."

I laughed at the way he said it.

"You're right about that," I said. "She's a mutt like you and me."

"Good thing she was," Al said.

"Why's that?"

"That's the stuff that connects us, you know? That's why we get along."

The agent came to the counter and I approached her and showed her my ticket.

"My brother and I are on this flight together," I told her, "but we're in different rows. Any way we could sit together?"

I told her Al's row and she looked at him and then looked at her screen and shook her head. "I'm sorry," she said.

"We haven't seen each other since we were kids," I said. I showed her the screen of my phone. It was a picture our mother took the first time we met. We have our arms around each other, holding each other tight, as if we'd known each other forever, holding each other tight in case someone was going to come and try to pry us apart. My face is beaming, a bright smile, wide eyes, the way only a child can look, except I was almost sixteen, a little younger than Sara is now. Al was more cautious, more reserved, smiling but not with abandon. He wasn't sure. Not about me. His caution was directed toward the camera, behind it, to the person holding it. Our mother. At that moment I didn't care. There's only the two of us in the photo, my brother and me. Who cares who took it and why we hadn't known about each other. We were together. "We haven't seen each other since then," I said.

She smiled, looking at the image on the phone. You couldn't help but smile. She went back to the screen. She looked at my ticket and tore it up. "I've got you," she said and printed a new ticket, in the middle seat next to Al. I went back and sat in the waiting area and kept quiet.

We boarded and Al didn't say anything when I sat next to him. That was all right, he didn't need to talk; I only wanted to be there if he felt the urge. He looked at the small oval window, at the lights on the runway, maybe the bay off in the distance and the ocean beyond that. That's how far away he was.

"Maybe we should have stayed," I said, "visited more of those saints you're so fond of."

"I need to get back anyway," he said.

"When's the last time we took a vacation?"

He shrugged but was still out past the runway, past the bay, somewhere past the ocean. "Vera was alive. We drove up to that cabin in Canada."

"House, not a cabin. We drove up to Nova Scotia. Had that amazing house there, right on the water. Remember?"

"I remember," Al said. "What town was that in?"

"You don't remember?"

"I don't remember."

I started laughing. "Another saint. Saint Andrews. You don't remember?"

He started laughing. "I don't remember that at all. We had a nice house, I remember that much. We looked right out to the lighthouse."

"On Saint Andrews Harbour," I said.

"I give up."

"We were going to go over to Halifax, remember, but never made it."

"Mom kidnapped Sara."

"That's right." We'd left Sara with our grandmother and then our mother came and offered to take care of her for a couple of hours and then ran off with her. Grandma called in a panic. She wanted to call the cops. Instead, we drove back as fast as we could. It took almost eight hours.

"Where was she?" Al said, not remembering that part either.

"Some guy's apartment. Her connect, I guess. I can't even remember how we found her. I remember you barging in, though, almost like I thought you were going to today."

Al smiled, remembering. He was back. We were back, the way we'd been before his hard drive went missing, even the way before Vera died, back in our old way of talking, old way of connecting, back the way we should be.

"I was probably afraid Mom was teaching Sara how to tie off," Al joked.

"She should have left her alone, the way she left us."

"She didn't leave me alone," Al said. "I was the one raised by her, technically. You got lucky, you got Grandma."

"Did you see her as a kid?"

"Grandma would come to us. We never went to see her. Never."

"And Grandma never told me when she was going to see you. Never mentioned you at all. It was one big secret."

"Every family has them," Al said, and I let it go.

I'm like my dad, I guess. We can keep secrets. I don't remember much of the story of them being on vacation; I don't really remember them barging in to get me, but I do remember being with my grandmother in an apartment with a bunch of people. I remember they were having fun. I was probably having fun. I was with my grandmother, who I rarely saw. I remember my mother yelling at Dad afterward, when we got home. She yelled at him for days.

As for secrets, my father has another one he carries around, and we've only talked about it a couple of times. There's not much to say about it. He simply doesn't know.

He's never met his father, doesn't even know who he is. His mother never told him, and he doesn't want to find out. There are rumors that his biological father is still living in town. When I was younger I was desperate to find out who it was; I'd walk by every house and wonder if he was in it. I'd look at every old man and wonder if it was him, try to find some resemblance to my father, watch how they looked at him and wonder if it was blood recognition (whatever I thought that was), wonder why they didn't acknowledge him. Now I'm like Dad. I don't care. He's never been a part of his life, never been a part of mine, just some idea you have that's never going to amount to anything.

It seems that almost everybody in my father's life has either lied to him or left him, or both. His mother, father, wife, they were either gone from the beginning or gone when he needed them most. Maybe that's why he's never left, fiercely loyal to his town and his family. I'm not trying to make excuses for him, maybe offer an explanation. And if my father and uncle wind up on opposite sides of whatever's going on between them, I know it will destroy my father, and I suspect it will ruin them both. I also know which side I'm on, no matter what the facts are.

Al talked a little more about Canada, the house and the water and the little fishing we got in before we had to head back for Sara.

"We had a good couple of days, though, up in Canada," Al said.

"We could go back," I said. "Take Sara. Maybe go up this summer. We need to do something with Sara, only a couple more summers left."

Al went quiet again. I could almost see him changing, the old brother being replaced with the new version from the past few days.

"Maybe Mexico," he said. "I should go and look at my property."

"I've never been there," I said, and he didn't invite me. He disappeared into his phone and I took another crack at *McTeague*.

After a while, Al leaned over and showed me a photo of the lighthouse in Saint Andrews.

"You want to see some more?"

"Not with any people," I said.

"I know." He scrolled through his photos, and scrolled some more, and finally showed me another one, but it wasn't in Canada. It was his spot in Mexico, just an empty lot, a lonely place in the countryside.

"I thought you were going to build there," I said.

"I should have. I will. Maybe I'll go down and work on that for a while."

"I could help," I said.

"I want it done right," he joked.

He showed me a couple more pictures of the land, different views of the same spot. Then he scrolled again and I saw a rendering of a hotel, a CGI of a beautiful building with a columned entryway and two stories of rooms stretching in both directions.

"What's that?" I said.

"An investment," Al said. "Of my father's. I gave him some money and he gave me a picture."

"Where's that?"

"Nowhere. It was supposed to be in Mexico City. He told me he had this great opportunity on this land, perfect for a hotel, he told me. He's not going to build it. I should have known. If he wanted money, he should have just come out and asked me. I won't see anything more than this picture. The worst of it is, he doesn't even need the money. It's amazing we turned out the way we did," he said. I didn't say anything. He scrolled past the image of the hotel and back to his land. "You should have bought the property next to me," he said. "We could both be down there."

"I can't see myself there," I said, "Not with Sara, not now, anyway."

"I could be there right now," he said. "I'm tired of all of this. I think I could leave and never look back. America's done. Everything seems like it's going backward and downhill at the same time."

"And you think Mexico is better?"

"Mexico can only get better; America's only going to get worse. Besides, where I am there's nothing to do but fish and mind your own business. I could build my house and keep to myself, and no one will know what I'm doing or care. I can do whatever the hell I want."

"You pretty much do that now," I said.

He shook his head in disagreement. "I don't want to be cold anymore. It's snowing back home right now. March is the worst. You're sick of winter and spring's still far away."

"The snow won't last," I said. "Better days are ahead."

"I don't know about that," he said, sounding the way he had for the last few years, ever since Vera. We thought he was improving, and maybe he was over it all, maybe it was just a momentary thing. Maybe I triggered him with the talk about our trip to Canada, maybe he saw a photo he shouldn't have, or maybe you never get over it. Who could? You could see the sadness come over him, like a shadow stretching across him, obscuring him and taking him into darkness. I closed the book and sat there, just in case he wanted to say anything, anything at all. He put his head back against the headrest and closed his eyes. I sat there and waited for my brother to return.

I texted Sara that we had landed. She texted back an article from yesterday's paper. At least it was good news. One of the Berling cops was suspended for "complaints of sexual assault of a minor." There wasn't more information, which made me fill in some blanks with assumptions and worries.

"Please tell me it wasn't you who made the complaints," I texted back.

"Ha. No. I know the girl, but I had nothing to do with it."

I showed the article to Al.

"That's one," he said. Turns out the other would be suspended the next day as part of an "ongoing investigation into criminal activity." It didn't explain why they'd be after us, or on whose behalf, but at least they'd been given a message. Maybe somebody had our backs for a change.

There was an inch or two of snow on the ground covering the grass and the fields as we drove home, enough to make it all seem different, as if everything had changed while we'd been away, like the furniture in a room had all been changed. It was probably just the jet lag. Nothing had changed.

"You want some breakfast?" I asked Al.

He shrugged and then nodded.

"In or thru?"

"Thru."

I found a drive-thru and ordered a couple of egg sandwiches and coffees. I handed Al his coffee and he looked disappointed. I knew why.

"In the glove box," I told him.

He opened it and found a small bottle of whiskey. He took the lid off his coffee and the steam rose and drifted between us in the car. He blew the steam away and kept blowing until maybe the coffee was cool enough and then took a few sips, cringing with each one, until he got the liquid low enough that he could add his whiskey.

"I don't know how you can drink it otherwise," he said.

"I don't know why you bother with the coffee," I said.

"You know why."

"Yes, I do," I said.

He took the lid off my coffee and let it cool while I drove and then Al unwrapped one of the sandwiches and handed it to me. I would have preferred to have gone someplace and sat down and eaten at a table, but there's a distinct pleasure in eating while you're driving, especially breakfast. It helps you wake up and makes you feel like you've got things to do, things that need your attention and can't wait. It makes you focus and gives you time to think and prepare yourself. I tried to think about what I was going to do about Al, what I was going to do if he handed over that hard drive, what I was going to do if my own brother was planning to betray me. It was hard to think that way when he was sitting there next to me, making sure my coffee was cool enough to drink, taking the sandwich from me and handing me the coffee with the lid back on, the tab turned up so I could get at it. Nothing had changed, I tried to tell myself, even though everything seemed to contradict the idea.

"Are we good, you and me?" I finally said. "I mean, you're not going to kill me or anything, are you?"

"We're good, for now," he said. Any other time I would have known he was joking. "There's still some questions that have to be answered."

"Well, you let me know if I can help. You know I'd do anything for you."

Al took another bite of his sandwich and looked out the window.

"I was looking for you at Bishop's Corner the other day," I said.

"I haven't been there in five years, I bet. Why'd you go there?"

"I don't know. Somebody told me to try there."

"They had you chasing a different me," he said.

Al finished his sandwich and drank his coffee. The snow had piled up another inch or so as we got closer to home. I wondered if I'd need to plow the drive when I got there, wondered if Sara would have shoveled the walk at least, wondered if she'd let Zeno play in the snow, roll around in it the way he likes, turning over and working his back into it.

"You remember that March snow . . ."

"I don't want to talk about the past," Al said. "You only talk about the past, you ever notice that?"

"I don't think that's true," I said. "Besides, we banked a lot of good times together. They're worth remembering."

"Not all the time. Not today, anyway."

We rode the rest of the way in silence and I thought that whatever Al decided was going to be determined without me. I didn't know what to think, but I wasn't optimistic. If I didn't know soon, I'd have to take the direct route with him, ask him straight out and see where that got us. About the time you have a plan in mind, have a course figured out, that's about the time something comes along you don't expect.

I pulled into Al's drive. There wasn't enough snow to plow. It would all melt during the day. Al hesitated before getting out.

"What are you doing today?" I said.

"I should show my face down at the store," he said. "Maybe I'll do that this morning and then go back to sleep."

"You should stay awake as long as you can, isn't that what they say?"

"I don't know," he said. He grabbed his bag from the back seat and opened it.

"Would you do me a favor?" he said. "Hang on to this for a couple of days for me." He took the hard drive out of his bag and handed it to me.

Lie, steal, kill. Those are the three elements of most criminal enterprises. Everybody lies, most people steal (or have stolen), very few people kill. I've done a little of the first, some of the second, but none of the third. That was a red line. And it's not out of fear of getting caught (most murders go unsolved—look it up), it's something else, some foundational element in our species. We're hard-wired to avoid it, mostly. Don't get me wrong, we don't have a problem with violence (clearly), but even with all the mass shootings and gun violence, murders are still remarkably rare (the US doesn't even rank in the top fifty countries of most murders per capita). "Few men get killed," Dashiell Hammett wrote in 1925, "most . . . get themselves killed." It was true a hundred years ago and it's still true. The overwhelming odds are that you'll get yourself killed falling down, or your heart gives out, cancer, dementia, you name it, there are plenty of ways for your body to kill you, and that's much, much more likely than somebody else doing it. And while you might think you want to kill somebody, someone who's wronged you, stood in your way, offended you, those thoughts remain almost entirely unacted upon. Most people have figured out that you can get what you want in life relying on lying and stealing; murder, on the other hand, has a good chance of taking away all the things you wanted. That was my opinion, anyway. Then again, you should always test your opinions.

I went home. The sidewalk was shoveled and Sara was already gone; her car tracks were in the unplowed driveway. I went inside and let Zeno greet me. He liked to run and bring me toys whenever he saw me and I let him bring some of his favorites, a knotted piece of rope, a small plastic ball with handles on it, and a stuffed squirrel -type thing that Sara gave him that has its ears chewed off and its tail barely hanging on, but Zeno maybe loves that toy the best. They all wound up at my feet and then he wanted to go outside. He went to the door and I told him to wait and he dropped his butt to the ground and waited. I texted Fitz and told him I'd be at the bar in a while and took Al's hard drive down to the safe and put it inside. He knew I couldn't do anything with it; maybe it was his way of telling me he wasn't going to do anything with it either. I tried to think it through, but gave up and went upstairs and put my boots on and Zeno was still waiting at the door, his ass still planted on the ground, still in the same spot. I opened the door and said, "Go on," and Zeno took off running.

There were four deer standing in the snow in the backyard and Zeno ran at a full sprint, his body moving quickly and smoothly over the ground. You can really see the greyhound in him when he runs, his body contracting and extending like an efficient spring, his forelegs digging hard and pushing well past his hind legs, all four legs off the ground with each stride when he's in full gallop. The deer stood frozen for a moment, their heads up straight and alert as they watched Zeno race toward them, and then they quickly bounded out of the yard and back into the woods. Zeno stopped where the invisible fence marks the property line. He patrolled the perimeter for a while, maybe hoping the deer would try to come back. Satisfied that everything was safe, he found a spot in the snow and dropped to his back and wriggled back and forth, kicking his legs with happiness as he rubbed himself in the snow.

There's a lot of deer in the neighborhood, but they usually stay out of the yard. Zeno keeps a close watch. We're surrounded by woods, but you see them on the road, standing on the pavement and eating grass they could eat safely just a few feet away. Whenever I see them on the property I always wish I had a gun, thinking I'd shoot one. I'm not sure I could. Whenever I see them on the road, I always worry about hitting one. Al had one come through his passenger window one time; the doe smashed her head right through the glass. I've never hit one, not head-on, anyway. We were coming back from a collection one evening and one ran out in front of us, and I reflexively hit the brakes and clipped the back legs with the left front of the car. The deer went down and struggled to get back up. I stopped the car, and Al and I watched it for a while as it rose in the ditch and tried to drag itself out but couldn't and went down again. It tried a couple of times.

"Maybe we should call somebody," I said.

"Who?"

"I don't know. Animal Control? The sheriff? Somebody we know with a gun."

Al looked around. The road was empty. The deer was struggling, but was now tired and barely even able to get up on her front legs. Al went to the back of the car and got the lug wrench from where the spare was stowed. I stood and watched as he walked up to the deer. The deer was calm, not frightened by Al's presence at all, as if Al was there to help. Al gripped the wrench and swung it in a quick, powerful arc, landing it right at the top of the deer's skull, dropping it dead in the ditch. Al wiped off the end of the wrench in the grass and came back and put it back next to the spare. He got into the passenger side and I started to drive. I couldn't say anything, thinking I might cry if I opened my mouth. Finally, I told Al, "I couldn't have done that."

"You could if you had to," he said. "And it had to be done."

I stayed with Zeno outside for almost half an hour, then went inside. Zeno caught up with me as I neared the door and pushed his way past me and went in and laid down on his bed. I went upstairs and showered and shaved and headed down to the Flying F.

Fitz had already started on the books by the time Zeno and I got there, which annoyed me. He was the owner and I was an employee, technically, but it still annoyed me. I wanted to get back into my routine, get back to the way things used to be, and now he was disrupting what little normalcy I had going for me. Besides, I told him I'd be in.

"I said I'd be in," I told him. Zeno found a table to curl up under but kept his eyes on me as I went to the bar.

"I know. I just thought I'd give you a head start. I can finish it up, if you want." Fitz had a cup of coffee next to him getting cold.

"Might as well see it through," I said and got a seltzer. There weren't any limes cut. I brought the coffee over and heated up Fitz's cup and set the empty coffee pot down on the table. Fitz left his table for a second and a few minutes later the kid came back with a small plate of sliced limes.

"You ever find Al the other day?" Fitz said.

"He always turns up sooner or later," I said, "But he wasn't at Bishop's Corner."

"Sorry for the bad tip."

"It didn't turn out all bad," I said. "I saw somebody else there. Maybe you know the guy. He said he might be buying the Flying F."

"He's mistaken," Fitz said.

"He doesn't think so. He also doesn't know about our terms of sale. I have to be notified of any offers and ten business days to counter. You remember that part of our agreement, right?"

"There haven't been any offers. Don't jump to any conclusions."

"I didn't jump. The guy handed them to me on a platter, couldn't wait to tell me he was taking over."

"He's over his skis, Peck. He asked if I was interested and I gave him some ridiculously high number, and that's the last I heard about it."

"You talk to about it?"

"I haven't yet, no. It's not a thing, Peck, not even close."

"Maybe your friend at Bishop's Corner talked."

"That's his problem, then. Because nothing's happening. I'm not selling, Peck."

"You named a price."

"No one would buy it at that price, not even you."

He looked up from his table and knew that he shouldn't have said it. I was already in a mood, jet-lagged and cranky, and then he has to start in on the books and then start in on me. I looked over at Zeno. He was comfortable, eyes closed, body relaxed, and I thought how nice it must be for him. I should have gotten up and left, but that would have meant waking Zeno and leaving Fitz with his remark. I looked back at Fitz.

"When we first got Zeno he was mouthy," I said. "He snapped at me a couple of times, especially when we were playing, got overexcited maybe, or bossy. Anyway, he snapped at me with that big mouth of his and caught me a couple of times on the hand. Drew blood. You ever been bitten by a dog, Fitz?"

"No," he said and looked over at Zeno still sleeping under the table.

"It hurts like hell. And makes you mad. Mad at the dog, you know. I didn't like it, and I didn't want it to happen to Sara. So we tried the usual stuff they tell you to do, distract him, make a loud noise when they bite you so they know it hurts, but nothing worked. We tried it a good while and then one day he was playing rough and Zeno bit Sara. Maybe he didn't mean to, you can't really tell what a dog's thinking, you know, but he bit her when she was trying to play with him and caught her thumb bad. You can't have a mouthy dog, especially not with your daughter. So you know what I did to solve it?"

"No," he said, starting to get nervous.

I called Zeno to me and told him to "stand," then took his leash. He didn't look like a greyhound now; he looked like a German Shepherd. The way he was standing showed off his muscular shoulders and back, and his broad head and strong jaw pointed directly toward Fitz, his eyes steady on him. I took his leash and stood next to Zeno; he was calm and quiet and still, but never took his eyes off Fitz.

"I cried when I did it, Fitz. Because we love Zeno, you know. And he's a good dog. Only he was a little mouthy there at first. So I figured out what to do, a last resort approach, and it made me cry, but it worked. He stopped being mouthy. You want to see what I did?"

"You can tell me," Fitz said.

"It's probably better if I show you. What I did was give him one good crack to his mouth," I said and picked up the coffee pot from the table and hit Fitz square in the fucking jaw with it. It knocked him out of his chair and onto the floor and Zeno looked at him and took a step toward Fitz.

"You ever been bitten by a dog, Fitz?"

He said something, maybe it was the word "no." It was hard to tell. I went over to the table and looked at his phone, his messages mostly, scrolling through until I found what I was looking for. I forwarded some stuff to my phone. Maybe Fitz was sloppy, maybe he was forgetful, the way most people are with crap on their phone, or maybe he was hanging on to it to use later, or for security. I didn't care; I was simply happy that it was still there. I put the phone back on the table and picked up the deposit bag for the bank and took Zeno by his leash and went to the truck.

I like Fitz; I like him more than most people in town, but I didn't cry over it, not the way I had with Zeno. It had to be done.

I don't know if any of that is true. I can't say for certain, but I can't imagine my father doing any of that. I saw Fitz soon after. He had a swollen jaw, but he said he'd had a tooth pulled. As for Zeno, I know for a fact that most of what he says he told Fitz never happened. Zeno was a little mouthy when we first got him, but he never bit me hard enough to draw blood. I think he grew out of it. My father would never hit Zeno the way he says, not with me around, anyway. He did cry over Zeno, though. He used to let him out at night for his final pee, and one night Zeno tangled with a porcupine and got about eight quills stuck in his face. I wanted to take him to the vet immediately, but Dad called Al and Al came down and Dad held Zeno while Al extracted the quills with a pair of pliers. I think Zeno bit both of them during that mess, but they weren't mad at him, and again, he didn't bite them hard enough to make them bleed. But Dad cried when it was done, cried more out of relief, sorry for what had happened to Zeno and the pain the dog was in, the way Dad would cry whenever I got hurt or felt bad. That's who he is. I don't know why he wants to portray himself otherwise, but I can guess.

When I came home from school, Dad and Zeno were in the living room, both asleep. Zeno got up and greeted me and my father opened his eyes, still groggy from the red-eye. I started to leave the room, to let him sleep.

"How was school?"

"Fine. How was Uncle Al?"

He sat up and Zeno went over and put his big head on Dad's knee, looking for a nose rub.

"Strange," he said. "Sometimes it was normal, though. That was the weirdest part."

"How was he about the drive? I mean, after."

"Irrational. But maybe he's over it. I don't know. But look . . ." He reached behind him under the cushion and showed me a hard drive. "He gave it to me. I don't know why, maybe he trusts us again. I don't know."

"That's very weird."

"Well, he knows I can't access it."

"What are you going to do with it?"

"Nothing. Put it back in the safe and wait. Al told me to hang on to it for a few days. So here it is."

"Maybe he's having second thoughts," I said.

What I didn't tell him was that I'd already seen Al. He came and met me after school, storming up to me and my friend Hanna like he wanted to fight.

"Is this Kelly?" he said, getting right up in her face.

"No," I said, "and stop acting like a lunatic."

Hanna knew Al. Everyone knows Al from the hardware store or wherever, but you usually don't see him foaming at the mouth like that.

"Don't worry, Hanna," I said, "he's mad at me about something, but he's harmless. I think. You're not going to hurt my friend Hanna, are you?"

He calmed down.

"No," he said. "I just need to talk to you."

"I'll be with you in a second," I said and waited until he retreated to his car. We could still see him standing there, though, impatient. Maybe going manic. I apologized to Hanna and told her to forget about it, which she's very good at, by the way, and then I walked across the street to Al's car. He waved at me hurriedly to get in and I opened the passenger door and sat down. He started the engine and I told him that I had my car at school and he turned the engine off and didn't look at me, but searched through the crowd still leaving school.

"I need to know about Kelly," he said.

"What do you need to know?"

"Everything. Who she is, where she is, and what she was doing with my drive."

"She's a friend of mine. I don't know where she is, and she was trying to do me a favor."

"What sort of favor?"

"Don't you know?"

"I want to hear it from you."

"I was told that there was information about Dad on your drive. I wanted to see for myself."

My uncle didn't say anything. He looked as if he might want to, his mouth churning his lips in small motions for a few seconds before he stopped, like an engine that can't turn over. I waited to see if maybe he'd try again, but he had gone quiet.

"Is there, Al? Is there stuff on your drive?"

"Where did you hear that?"

"I've told you. There are a lot of people who talk. I don't listen to most of it, but this I heard loud and clear. And I wasn't going to wait around to find out whether it was true or not. You want to tell me if it is?"

"It's more complicated than that." Quiet again. "You need to stay out of it, though. This is between your father and me."

"And me. Whatever's between you also involves me. You can't be mad at him."

More quiet. "There's a lot going on, Sara. I can't tell you anything about it right now. But everything's going to be all right, I think. I'm working on it. Tell me exactly what you heard."

So I told him. Corrupt business practices, falsifying business records, money laundering, all of it. "And you had the receipts on your drive and were going to hand them over to the DA, and when you did, you'd get immunity and Dad would get arrested."

"For one thing," Al said, "that's not how it works, and for another, those kinds of rumors have been circulating since you were born, almost."

"It doesn't mean they aren't true now, though," I said. "Your drive was right there on your desk."

"What does that mean? Nothing."

"Then why were you so upset about it?"

"You and your friend stole from me, and then tried to burn down the place."

"We didn't have anything to do with the fire," I told him.

"You didn't?"

"Absolutely nothing."

Al thought for a second and then said, "I need to go see somebody."

"Who?"

"Don't worry about anything. Stick with what you know, Sara. I think I know a way out of this."

"You're the one who's in trouble, not Dad," I said.

"Everything's all right. Now tell me more about your friend Kelly."

"She's smarter than I am. If I can't figure something out, chances are she can, and if she can't she definitely knows someone who can."

"Like the guy in Oakland."

"Like the guy in Oakland."

"Who else?"

"Everybody. But she's not the one who told me, if that's what you're thinking. She knows other stuff, like if you ever want something you can't find, she'll find it."

"I hope I'm done with your friend Kelly," Al said. "I hope we'll be done with all of this soon. Anyway, I should go. Don't tell your dad about this, okay?"

I don't know why I agreed to it; I had no intention of keeping it from him. But then, sitting there with my father, I knew I wasn't going to say anything. He was getting almost as pissed as Al. Maybe it was the jet lag, the drain of dealing with Al's lies and deceit. It was still bad between them. I had tried to fix it, was still trying to fix it, but neither one of them was making things any easier.

"I know who told you about Al," my father said. "Maybe she's wrong. Or maybe she's lying about it, you know?"

"Forget the source," I said.

"I can't do that. Your source is a liar. She lied to me, she lied to you, she's lied to just about everyone we know. And she hates me. She might have told you something just to mess with me."

"She doesn't hate you, Dad. She loves you."

"That's a funny way of showing it."

"She loves you, just not in the way you want."

"The way I want. The way I want was simple. To be honest, to be faithful, not to lie and cheat, and not to run off with someone else. You remember the kind of love she had?"

"I remember, Dad. But that doesn't mean she's wrong about Al. You didn't talk about it with Al?"

"I gave him plenty of opportunity. He didn't take it. Maybe there's nothing there. I don't know. But between the two of them, between your mother and my brother, my money's on my brother. As far as I know, he's never lied to me, as far as I know he's never cheated me."

"Point taken, Dad. Just be careful."

"You want to go to Canada this summer?"

"You getting rid of me?"

"No. Something I was talking with Al about on the flight. Maybe the three of us going up there this summer. A vacation."

"We'll see," I said, thinking my father was removing himself from reality right in front of my eyes.

I didn't hear from my mother for almost two years after she left. She had run off with some guy I didn't even know—didn't know his name, didn't know what he looked like—and fucking disappeared. For two years I didn't get a birthday card from her, Christmas card, any card at all, not a phone call, text, email, not one single word from her to let me know where she was and what she was doing, and not a single word asking about me and how I was doing, what I was doing. Nothing. I can't tell you how horrible I felt, horrible about myself and what part I played in her leaving. I hated her, but I also hated myself. My father saved me. We never talked about it, but he altered his life to spend more time with me, driving me to school in the morning and picking me up afterward, always there to make me dinner, breakfast in the morning, whatever I needed and whenever I needed it. And if Dad wasn't there, Al was. Al would always bring me something, cookies, fruit, flowers, a book he thought I might like, a tennis racket, a fishing rod, a set of golf clubs, serious stuff, goofy stuff, a delicate bird's nest he found on the ground, a hawk feather, a deer antler, but always something. It was always something to distract me, something he and I could talk about. And don't forget, he was grieving at the time, carrying a pain worse than mine. It was tough in the beginning, though, when Al would disappear for a few days, usually Friday afternoon until Monday morning, and Dad knew he was on a binge. I'm sure I saw him drunk, but I don't really remember, then I think Dad talked to him, told him he couldn't be around me if he was drinking all the time. It was a bright line in the sand and Al had a choice to make. Luckily, he chose me.

I know the drinking was bad for him, but I liked that version of Al. He was still sad, but it could be covered up with alcohol, patched over long enough for him to get happy—or at least seem happy—sing silly songs, laugh for a few minutes. After he stopped drinking he became a robot, acting like a human but not being one. He was devoted to me, to being there for me, with or without my father, but there was an anger there, always just below the surface. We were all angry; I think we had enough rage between the three of us to set the whole state on fire and have it burn for weeks, but we also had fun.

Al took me to get my ears pierced, would take me to get my nails done. Sometimes the three of us would go together, and once we all got mani-pedis together. Al has the hands of someone who has spent a lot of hours working with them, rough and worn, with dirt rubbed into the creases and under the nails. My father initially refused to get his feet done; Al got his toes painted, the same color as mine. It was still fun, but when Al was drinking, it was a party. He liked to joke with the women who worked at the salon, get them laughing as they worked on him. And he tried to get them drunk. He always arrived with a big metallic bottle with "Al's Hardware" printed in bold block letters, filled with something sugary and strong—gin and juice, rum and coke, tequila and Squirt—and he'd offer it to the girls, and a few of them would sneak drinks. And then the party started. There would be music, and maybe even dancing. Al with his painted toes, waltzing around the shop. I'm glad that he's not drinking anymore, but some days, even some weeks, that was the only fun we had.

I think that if the old Al had still been around, the Al I knew when Vera was still alive, none of this would have happened. *That* Al had the answers, or seemed to know what to do, could figure shit out. My father never could, at least not at this level. It was like a complex machine that needed to be fixed, and all my father could do was watch, not understanding how to stop it or how to repair it. My father only knew how to hand the tools to his brother, and after Vera died, Al didn't want anything to do with it anymore. He didn't care if the machine was broken, he didn't care if it ever got fixed, he didn't care about it at all. He was part of the machine, a broken gear snagged right in the middle.

My father and uncle did what they could for me, and I don't know if I would have made it without them, but as much as they did, it always ended up reminding me that they were trying their best to take the place of someone who wasn't there, refused to be there, who I didn't know how to reach, even if I wanted to.

I don't know if Dad knew where she was, maybe he didn't want to tell me. Maybe he didn't want to know. And I didn't want to know, and the more time that passed the more I didn't want to know. Let her be gone. Let her be really gone. I hoped that she was dead. I would dream about it at night, my brain twisting all sorts of fantasies of her being murdered, dying in a car crash, a dog or some other animal tearing at her throat, a building collapsing on her, her falling down a well and drowning, screaming in the middle of the woods where no one could hear or, in a different version, a crowd standing and paying no attention to her pleas for help. The dreams did not bother me in their violence or in the empty wish fulfillment, only in their frequency. I wanted to get to the moment when I wouldn't dream about her, wouldn't think about her, wouldn't have her take up any space in my mind at all. And then about the time I started to not think about her, she reached out.

"I hope you will let me explain myself, and won't be too mad at me," she emailed me out of the blue. I deleted the email but could almost re-create it here word for word, but I won't. It was a self-serving rationalization that tried to blame my father for what happened. I didn't care. I didn't care what she said or how she defended what she'd done. She had left me when I was thirteen and had gone into hiding like a coward. I read the email and immediately deleted it, didn't reply, didn't even tell my father about it.

She kept emailing me and I kept ignoring her, sometimes not even making it past the first sentence.

"There are things I want to tell you about me." Delete.

"I worry about you and your dad." Delete.

"You should . . ." Delete.

Finally, she stopped explaining and complaining and began the "just wanted to check in with you" emails, with that as the subject. I didn't even bother to open those. Straight to trash. Then she began asking questions, mostly about when I was a baby. "Do you still have that sweater my mother knitted for you?" Things like that. I didn't respond to those either, but she kept at it, reaching out once or twice a week.

Then she asked a very interesting question.

"Do you want to yell at me?" was the subject.

"I was going to write you to ask if we could try a fresh start," she wrote, "but I know that's a stupid question. Of course we can't. What I did to you can't be ignored. You can't ignore it, so maybe it would be better if you could confront it directly. Confront me. Can we meet somewhere, anywhere, and you can say anything to me, ask me anything, do anything short of beating me to a pulp (as much as you might want to)? Can we do that? I don't deserve to be a part of your life, but I would love to be any part, no matter how large or small, that you would allow. If you want me to have no part at all, I understand. Please let me know. Whenever you're ready." I sat on that for a week. There was not another email, and I found myself checking to see if she'd sent one. I didn't tell my father about any of this, mostly because there was nothing to tell him. I didn't tell him about all the other spam I was deleting, did I? But this one was different. It made me think. Did I want her to be part of my life? My father was still angry, so angry you couldn't mention her name around him, but I was getting over that. I had more important things going on. My mother wasn't part of any of it, and I didn't see how letting her back in would improve my life at all. Still, I thought about it.

Finally, I wrote back. "I could meet you after school or on the weekend. I would prefer after school. I promise I won't beat you to a pulp." She picked me up after school and we drove out of town to a diner where she figured no one would see us, especially Al and my father. My father would kill me, is about all I could think about the whole time. And the whole time at the diner was about half an hour. My mother had a coffee and I had a milkshake, and we sat and didn't talk. She was letting me set the tone and I didn't know what to say. I finished my shake and she paid and then drove me back, not all the way home, but close enough that I could walk.

"Would you do this again?" she asked as we got close to home.

"You want to?"

"I want to," she said. "More than you know. I want to any time you want."

"Okay," I said, and it came out flatter and more insensitive than I intended.

"Maybe we can talk next time. No pressure," she said, and then laughed.

"I'll work on it," I said.

"You don't have to," she said. "I'm serious. We can just sit. I'm fine with that. I'm just grateful that you agreed to meet. Really." I thought she might hug me and was glad she didn't try. I probably would have hugged her back. Instead, I got out of the car and walked up the hill to the house, glad that I'd seen her but realizing that I would have to deceive my father. I was seeing my mother behind his back, the way she had seen another man. Was I really going to do that to him?

"What the hell did you do to Fitz?" Al said. He hadn't even come in the door. He didn't even turn off his car lights; they just glared at us from the driveway.

"You leave your car running?" I said.

"I didn't think this would take long, and it wouldn't if you'd just tell me what's going on."

"Did you talk to Fitz?"

"Yeah."

"What did he tell you?" I said.

"He told me he had some dental work done."

"There you go."

"It's not like you to clock somebody," Al said.

"You usually get there first," I said. "At least come in so I can keep the cold out of the house."

Al stepped inside and I started to move out of the hallway, but he stayed put.

"What did he do?" Al said.

I turned around and saw that he wasn't mad as much as he was concerned.

"He pissed me off."

"Clearly. But how?"

"He got all smart about the bar, said he might sell it."

"That doesn't sound right," Al said.

"He denied it, sort of."

"What does that mean?"

"He said that somebody approached him and he put a high price on the place. He was dancing around the edges, not being straight, that much I know."

"He's always been straight with you, I thought."

"As far as I know," I said. "Everybody's got different ideas about things lately."

Al looked toward the floor for a second, then looked back at me.

"You shouldn't have done it, Peck," he said.

"You're one to talk."

"I'm serious. We're in enough trouble with Fitz as it is."

"What does that mean?"

"What? I don't know. I mean, if he's thinking about selling the bar behind your back, something must be going on."

"What's going on, Al?"

"I don't know," he said, looking back to the floor. "We might not find out now, though. Not with Fitz, anyway. You should see his jaw. He must have gone to the worst dentist in town."

"I'll see him tomorrow."

"It's not going to be business as usual, not with him now. You need to be careful."

"You think he'll do something stupid again?"

"I don't know. He'll either fall back in line or come back at you."

"Which way do you think he'll go?"

"Fitz? Fitz seems like the kind of guy who'll fall back in line, but I'm not so sure. Sometimes those are the kind of guys that will surprise you. The way you did with him. I bet he never would have thought that would happen, ever. It's not your way."

"It seemed like the only way to go," I said.

"I'm sure it did," Al said, "but that doesn't mean it was."

I watched him walk back to his car and drive off, the white staring lights finally turning their attention the other way.

"I have to go meet Mom," I told Dad. I told him every time. He didn't want to hear it, but it was better than lying to him. He would find out sooner or later, and I didn't want him to find out later, the way he did with my mother stealing and cheating on him. So I always told him. That's the way it was between us.

"I'll be here," he said from the couch, with Zeno lying down near him. "Call if you need to be rescued."

"And you'll come running?"

"No. I'll send Al. Or Zeno."

"I thought that was your father for a second when you drove up," my mother said when I sat down. We were at a pizza place in town. I didn't care who saw us anymore. I think she was more concerned with who might notice her, the way she looked around, glancing at everybody in the place to see if anyone was watching us. I thought it had to do with me; she didn't want to be seen with Peck's daughter. No one cared. No one was looking at us. "He should have at least got you a new car."

"It's fine," I said. "I wanted it. It's the only car I know. A trustworthy friend."

She didn't say anything. I didn't expect her to. The waitress came and handed me a menu and asked if I wanted anything other than water. I told her no and she left me alone with my mother thinking I should have ordered something.

"Nothing's happened," I said. "At least not what you said."

"Because you changed it," she said. "You changed the course of everything. You stepped in and stopped it from happening. For now, anyway."

"Al wasn't going to do anything," I said. "And he won't."

"He has to do something," she said with too much confidence. "He's in the middle of a three-pronged vice, if there is such a thing."

"There isn't," I said, matching her confidence.

"Still, you get my point. He has to answer to too many people. He has to do something. And soon."

"We'll see."

I was ready to leave, but the waitress came back and my mother ordered a pizza and a salad to share. We handed our menus to the waitress and she left me alone with my mother again.

"What does your father know?"

"He knows that I'm here," I said.

"That's not what I meant. I meant about what's going on."

"I haven't told him, if that's what you're worried about. But I will. I'll tell him before Al can do something."

"You can't," my mother said. "They'll know it came from me."

"What do I care?" I wanted to say, but I didn't. "It could come from Al," I said. "I'll talk to him."

"I shouldn't have said anything," my mother said. "I shouldn't have told you."

"It's too late for that."

We didn't say anything more about it and the pizza and salad came and my mother ate quickly and nervously, still looking around the room, like an animal worried about predators. That's the natural state of things, I suppose. Stress, nervousness, worry that someone's going to see you doing something, worry that someone's going to want what you have, want it bad enough to take it. You can't help but be nervous. I never really saw my father act that way, though, and not Al either, except for when Vera was real sick. Then it all went away, drained out of him along with everything else. I can't imagine him being nervous at all anymore, can't imagine him caring about what happened to him. I wondered if my mother knew what she was talking about, wondered if I could trust what she was telling me. She had lied to all of us before, maybe she was lying now, not warning us, but setting us all up for something we didn't know was coming.

She steered the conversation toward meaningless subjects, filling the silence with safe topics as she waited for the leftovers to be boxed and the check to appear.

"You sound like your father," she said.

"You say it as if it's a bad thing."

"It was just an observation," she said, "not a judgment. In fact, I like it. I like hearing your father in you. I miss him."

There must have been an eyeroll on my side of the table.

"I know you don't believe me, but it's true. I didn't stop loving him, Sara; I just couldn't be around him anymore. Actually, that's not true. I couldn't be around Al, which was sort of the same thing."

"I wouldn't blame Al," I said. "You made your own choice."

"I don't blame him. But he's a big part of why I left. I don't blame him—he'd lost Vera, and I understand all of that—but he took up so much of our energy, so much of our lives. We devoted all of our time to him, you remember, and he was so broken and angry. And then he started drinking—maybe you don't remember that—and drinking all the time. Your father would get up in the middle of the night and go pull Al out of bars, sometimes out of jail. Al would be gambling, or fighting, or both. He was a mess, and I'm not blaming him, but it was a lot, a lot every day, a lot for your father, and a lot for me. Al took up all of our time and energy so there wasn't anything left, no space for the rest of us. And he had so much anger, it spilled out everywhere and it infected the rest of us. Maybe you didn't see it in your dad, but it was there, like a mad dog thrashing around in a room, that you couldn't help but get bit by it and catch the anger yourself. That's how it was; that's part of the reason I left. We had devoted so much time, your dad and I, to help Al get better, that our relationship got damaged and we didn't have time or space to help it get better."

I didn't believe it when she said it, and I believe it less now.

"You had enough time to find someone else," I said. "And enough space to sneak around behind our backs." But I wasn't angry. I didn't have the time or space for that rage anymore; it wouldn't burn the state, maybe not even the corner of Al's garage.

I drove home convinced that I would never see her again, never have another conversation with her, that I could ignore her texts and emails and whatever messages she wanted to send my way, but I wouldn't sit down at a table with her and let her speak like that again. When I went inside, Dad was still on the couch, reading something he'd pulled off the shelf, and

Zeno was still lying on the floor next to him. They both looked up at me as I stepped into the room. Zeno put his head back down and closed his eyes.

"How's your mom?"

"The same," I said. "Which is not a compliment."

"It's good that you saw her," he said. "She should be a part of your life, if you want. She is your mother."

"I know who she is," I said.

I knocked on the door of the Flying F and Fitz answered.

"Where's the kid?" I said.

"He didn't work out. Where's Al?"

"He's working on something else."

"On Thursday?"

"He's got another obligation. Don't worry, I can grab an extra for him if you want."

"That's all right," Fitz said.

I walked toward the bar.

"You got any coffee on."

"Just. You want me to get it?"

"I'll get it."

I poured a couple of cups and brought them over to the table where Fitz was sitting. I put a cup of black coffee in front of him and set mine across the table and sat down in front of it.

"Cream?" Fitz said. "You always take it black."

"Time for a change," I said.

We drank our coffee and I waited.

"You know who Alexander Litvinenko is?" I asked.

"No," Fitz said.

"How about Pyotr Verzilov?"

"No."

"Ever heard of Ivan Kivelidi?"

"You joining the Russian mafia, Peck?"

"Just wondering if you know about them."

"I don't know anything about them."

"Kivelidi was a Russian banker who had his office phone laced with poison. Verzilov was poisoned a few years ago with a substance that leaves the body almost immediately after doing its work and is almost impossible to detect. They don't know how it was administered. Litvinenko was a specialist in organized crime and accused Vladimir Putin of operating a 'mafia state.' They poisoned his tea."

"By 'they' you mean Putin."

"Some people drink tea," I said. "Some people drink coffee. Am I right?"

Fitz looked at his coffee and then looked at me.

"You think this is not happening?" I said. "You think I'm making it up? Maybe you think this shit only happens in spy movies. They stab a guy in the calf with an umbrella; they break into a hotel room and spray poison on a guy's underwear; they follow a guy into an embassy and hack his body to bits and carry it out in bags. That happens every day, Fitz. And you know what happened to the guys who did that? Nothing. Everybody shrugged their shoulders and the world moved on. And that was for important men, men trying to do good in the world. Do you think anyone is going to care one tiny bit when they find you slumped over?"

He sat there wide-eyed and disbelieving, and when he started to get up out of his chair, almost involuntarily, I only had to give him a soft shove to get him to sit back down. I took his phone from the table and put it in my pocket.

"We're going to sit here a few more minutes," I told him. "Maybe you still think it can't be real, that it's some sort of fantasy of mine. I'll tell you a fantasy, that you could get between my brother and me. That you could ever turn him against me. But maybe you think it will still work out for you. Maybe you think you know how it works, know more about it than I do. So we'll sit here a few more minutes and see who's right and who's not, what's real and what's not.

"None of this should have happened," I continued. "I trusted you. There's not too many people in the world who I trust, but you were one of them. You had a nice setup here. If you had come to me, maybe we could have worked things out, found some satisfaction for you. What did you want? Money? I would have given you more. Maybe you wanted to be higher up. We could have had that. I'd have given you anything you wanted. But over time, it wouldn't have worked. That's the problem, you're not satisfied. You're never satisfied. I don't blame you. That's what we're all taught. It's the American dream, isn't it? Except it's not. Everyone all over the world dreams of having a better life. The American dream is to be never fulfilled, never quenched, to never be satisfied, and always want more. I give you three, you want five; I give you five, you want ten; and on and on. No matter what I do, given enough time, you start to resent me, you think that I'm to blame for your unhappiness, that you can do what I do, maybe if you have my position that will make you happy. Maybe if you have more and more you'll be happy. Are you happy now, Fitz? Are you fucking happy now?"

Fitz sat and took a last look at the money in front of him.

"It was Bishop," he said. "You have to believe me. It was Bishop."

I shrugged. "Same difference at this point. Maybe he set the cops on us, but you knew about it, and after that, you went along. Maybe it would have turned out different if you'd been the one making the decisions. You have to think about that, Fitz. Think about how maybe it could have worked out if Bishop had listened to you. Instead, you let him drive this thing. And this is where we are. It won't be long now. You remember the guy before me, Mr. Potato Chip? Had a heart attack after his morning coffee. That's all it is, Fitz. I'm not telling you that's what happened; I'm telling you that's what's going to happen."

I took his phone out of my pocket and went through it, deleting some stuff from it, things no one needed to see or know. I wiped the phone with a handkerchief and put it back on the table and looked over at Fitz, sitting there with a resigned panic, trying to be calm as he realized what was happening, the imminence of it all.

"It's too late now. Absolutely too late to do anything about it. Even if you could get to a hospital in time, even if they had the antidote, even if I had the antidote on me; it's too late." I got up and took the deposit bag Fitz had prepared. I left the rest of the money on the table. Let him look at it some more. Let him see what he wanted more of, what he was willing to risk everything for, and what he wouldn't be getting. I finished my coffee and took his cup and went behind the bar and washed them and put them in a plastic to-go bag and walked out the door. It's a zero -sum game. I tried not to play it that way, but that's how everyone else plays it, so that must be how they fucking like it.

That's my father's version of events. I don't believe it. I believe my father is an honest man and I don't think he would lie, unless he felt it was absolutely necessary, unless he was protecting someone he loved, like his brother. I don't believe my father would poison someone; I don't even believe he would know how, not the way he described it. Al would know. Al would do it. The only surprising thing was that he didn't do it earlier. Maybe that's why he was stalling, buying time until he figured it out, how to make the poison, or that's how long it took him to get it. That's what he was doing with his hard drive out the night before I took it, he was buying the poison, paying for it with his bitcoin or whatever, thinking he had all his tracks covered. I don't mean to go all headcanon / alt. facts on you, but this is how I think it happened. I think this is the truth:

Al and my father went to the bar, the way they always do on Thursdays, and Al pounded on the back door the way he always did. And Fitz answered.

"Where's the kid?" my dad asked.

Maybe Fitz told them the kid didn't work out, maybe the kid quit. It doesn't matter. There was no one else in the bar. Al and Fitz and my father spent a lot of mornings together, just the three of them, drinking coffee and counting money and getting ready for the day. The kitchen crew wouldn't come in for an hour or so, and even if they were there, they rarely came out to the bar. They had jobs to do. That's the way it worked.

But today was different.

Al got the coffee. My father was at the table with Fitz. Al poured a couple of cups and brought them over to the table where Fitz was sitting. He put a cup of black coffee in front of him and set another across the table in front of my father.

"Cream?" Fitz said. "You always take it black."

"Time for a change," my father said.

Al went back to the bar and poured himself a cup and came back and sat down. They drank their coffee and maybe they talked about dead Russians. It doesn't matter what they talked about. The important thing is who poured the coffee. My father was at the table with Fitz. I wasn't there, but I see it as clearly as if I were. Fitz is on one side of the table, drinking his coffee, and Al and my dad are on the other, waiting. There's money on Fitz's side, stacked and ready to be taken to the bank. Maybe Al taunted him. I don't think my father talked that way to people. I never heard it. And I can't imagine him talking like that to Fitz. They'd worked together for a long time; they were friends. If anyone talked to him that way, it would have been Al.

"You think this is not happening? You think I'm making it up?" That sounds like Al, not my father. He could at least describe it so it sounded like something he might say. It could be that my father wasn't even there yet, that Al went there early. He's telling you what Al told him, but changing it around, leaving Al out of it. Maybe it was just Al and Fitz, and my father came later, walked in and saw Fitz on the floor and called 911.

That way makes more sense, especially when you consider what happened after, what happened at Bishop's Corner, which, if the timing is correct, my father could not have been there. He was at the Flying F. Al was at Bishop's Corner. At least that's the rumor. All you have to do is look at a map and a clock. If my father and Al were both at Fitz's at the time my father says, Al can't be at Bishop's Corner. Al can only be at Bishop's Corner if he's at Fitz's earlier, which is before my father arrives. I know this, because I was at the house with my father. I remember him coming back from walking Zeno. So take that into account. And let me just say that my father wouldn't know how to get the kind of poison he describes, and he'd be terrified to come anywhere near it. Al worked at a hardware store; he could get poison easily enough, or get it online. Maybe ask someone else for it. My father wouldn't know the first thing about it and, even if he did, wouldn't have been able to go through with it. It couldn't have played out that way, not the way my father tells it. And then remember that it was Al who left for Mexico, and not my father, well, not right away. That was later.

Or else someone else was at Fitz's. Not Al and not my father. A larger conspiracy, involving a network of actors, including who Al and my father worked for. It was a criminal organization, after all, with all of the backstabbing and duplicitous maneuverings you see in the movies. This is possible. This is entirely plausible, but I can't say who it might have been. Al and my dad come into the bar, the way they always did, and both find Fitz on the floor. My father calls 911 and Al goes to Bishop's Corner. It could have happened that way. Then my father is protecting someone else.

Or it all happened exactly the way it's described in the official report. Heart attack. That's the truth, as far as the authorities are concerned, after all.

I could make up a hundred different stories, I guess, each as plausible and as wrong as the one my father pulled together. My point is not that I know anything, other than my dad can't be believed, at least in this one instance. You have to think about these things. You have to remember why my father is telling this the way he is. Everything has consequences. He'll get at the truth, but maybe only with a few lies.

I went back to the Flying F and called 911. Except I couldn't, not at first. When I saw Fitz on the floor, my hands started shaking and I could feel the sick rising in my gut. I hurried to the toilet and threw up. I splashed cold water on my face and called from the hallway, where I didn't have to look at him. Then I took the money off the table and put it in the bank deposit bag. Fitz was on the floor and I turned him over on his back and I felt his wrist and his neck for a pulse and leaned in to put my cheek near his mouth, doing whatever I thought should be done when you find someone on the floor when they shouldn't be there. I was all right then. It was over and all I had to do was wait for the ambulance and they'd take it from there.

The EMTs came through the door and rushed to Fitz and after a few seconds their actions slowed. They came over and said, "He's gone."

"I thought so," I said. "I came in to work and saw him there. I was afraid I was too late."

I called ██████ and told him how I found Fitz on the floor.

"The same thing happened at Bishop's," he said. "What are the odds of that?"

"The EMTs said heart attack for Fitz."

"That's what they said at Bishop's too. Not a chance. Not a fucking chance."

"I can't get a hold of Al," I said.

"What does he have to do with it?"

"I don't know. Maybe they got him too."

"Who's *they*?"

"I don't know. Do you?"

"I have an idea," he said.

I didn't believe him. He was bullshitting. Maybe I could make use of that.

"I have to find Al," I said.

"Be careful."

"You too."

"I don't have anything to worry about," he said, with a confidence that seemed presumptuous.

"Al's gone to Mexico," my father told me. "I have to go get him."

I didn't say anything. I didn't ask any questions, didn't ask for an explanation, and tried not to wonder why it was so important for my father to chase after him. Let Al go to Mexico, I thought, that would solve a lot of our problems. But that's how I saw it; I knew my father saw it differently and whatever I said wasn't going to change his mind.

He took me down into the basement and showed me the safe and told me the combination and had me open it. It was filled with cash, bundles of it, stacks of it, rows of it, more cash than you'd ever see in your life outside a bank.

"Don't get excited," my father said. "This isn't ours. We're just hanging on to it until Al comes back. But if someone comes looking for it, really comes after it, you know, give it to them. Don't ask any questions, just give it to them. You understand?"

I nodded but couldn't imagine ever opening the safe. I wanted it closed and out of my mind. No one was going to come, I thought, my dad and uncle will be back before then. My face must have shown what I was thinking.

"No one's going to come after it," he said. "Don't worry about that. They know to wait for me. This is just in case." He had me open it again, and then again, to show that I knew how. "It's only money," he said. "Remember that. Nothing to get worried about."

I stayed home as much as possible. I woke up, let Zeno out, and then went to school and came home during lunch and then again at the end of the day. I didn't feel comfortable away from home, away from the safe in the basement. I would go down and look at it and tell myself that I wasn't going to open it, that no one had opened it. No one had come inside the house and went down to the basement and opened it and taken everything. But the longer I looked at the closed safe, the more I began to wonder, then I had to open it, just to make sure. I kept it open only for a few seconds and then closed it again and made sure it was all locked up tight. It was stupid, I know, but it was the only way to stop thinking about it. I would do that in the morning before I left for school and then as soon as I came back. The door stayed open longer and longer, until I was not just looking at the money, but holding it, taking out the stacks and staring at them, dragging a thumb across the edges the way you see them do in the movies, as if they are counting a stack. It was then that I noticed a stack of pages in the back of the safe. It was this manuscript. Not at all of it, obviously. It was like a diary, but not really. I didn't know why my father would be writing it; maybe he wanted to set the record straight, or rewrite it, or have it as evidence. I didn't know. You hear about people leaving behind documents, just in case something happens to them. I didn't want to think like that. And I didn't want my father to get himself in trouble. So I took a magic marker through some of it, then I started adding pages. I thought he'd notice; I was hoping he'd notice. I really was. But he never said anything about the pages

I was putting there. Maybe he didn't notice. Maybe he just copied his new pages and stacked them on top of the old ones. Of course, this meant there was another copy somewhere, another hard drive I'd have to break into. Another thing I tried not to think about.

But I continued to make my way up and down the stairs to the safe, once in the morning and once at night. Zeno would follow me as far as the basement door and then wait, peeking his head across the threshold and giving me a "what the hell are you doing down there?" look when I started up the stairs. Even he knew it was stupid.

It wasn't entirely stupid, though. One night a car pulled into the drive and sat there for a good ten minutes. Zeno and I watched from the living room window. Finally, I put Zeno's leash on and walked out the door with him. I didn't take more than a couple of steps off the front porch when the car turned around and drove off. They were coming for the money, I thought. They were all going to come for it, and I wasn't going to give it to them. I didn't tell my father. He had enough to worry about.

I invited friends over after that, anyone who wanted to chill and watch a movie, do homework together, anything. Kelly would say she'd come, but bail at the last minute. I think she didn't like who else was coming. Maybe. I don't know. Sometimes, she's a mystery. She can be distant and cut off, and then very open and revealing. Especially when we're alone together. That's when she'd show me who she was, take me into her confidence. So I stopped inviting anyone else. When I told Kelly about the car she came over. She was wearing black leggings and a navy blue hoodie. And black Doc Martens that looked as if they'd been run over by a train. A lot. As soon as she closed the door, she unlaced the boots and tucked the laces inside the boots. "I didn't know whether to wear something to run in or something to fight in," she said. "So I opted for a little of both." She stood still and let Zeno sniff at her. She smelled good. "You have a gun?"

"You know how to use one?"

"I think we can figure it out," she said. "Morons use them all the time, don't they?"

"I don't think we have one," I said. "At least, I don't know where it would be. Besides, we have Zeno."

Kelly scratched Zeno under the chin and knelt down for him to smell her. Zeno leaned in close and gave her a quick lick right on the lips. Kelly didn't flinch or pull back. Instead, she kept her face still, maybe even leaned toward Zeno a little, as if inviting another lick.

"You have a dog?" I said.

"I wish. No dog, no drugs, no gun, no fun. I've got nothing to offer."

"That's not true at all," I said. "I need the company. I can't stay by myself like this."

We moved into the living room and sat on the couch, with Zeno curled between us. I was ready to move the conversation to different topics; Kelly was not.

"I hope they come," she said. "We'll find out who it is and get back at them."

"What would you do?"

"Nothing right away. We'd figure out a long game, some extended revenge, I think. I bet it's someone you know. Somebody else from school."

"I didn't recognize the car," I said.

"That doesn't mean anything."

"What if it's someone after my dad?"

"Then they don't know us. We could still go after them."

"They're not dumb high school kids," I said.

"Don't give them too much credit. They may not be high school, but they're still dumb. They drove into your drive, didn't they? If you had their license number we could find them. I hope they come back."

Kelly was fearless like that. I sort of hoped they'd come back now too, just to see what Kelly would do, what kind of revenge she'd scheme up, but they never did.

Kelly leaned back against the couch's armrest, stretching her legs out across the couch until they touched Zeno's side. He turned so she could scratch his belly with her feet. Kelly was new. She'd transferred from a private boarding school in January, trailing a steady stream of rumors. She'd been kicked out for drugging a fellow student; she'd assaulted the headmaster; she'd slept with one of the teachers; a lot of that stuff. People avoided her at first; she wanted to be one of those hold-by-the-edges-only types, but I didn't have time for that. It was a moth to the flame thing and she burned brighter than anyone else I knew, so I flew right in. What did I have to lose? We connected immediately.

"So what happened at your old school?" I asked her.

"It wasn't the place for me," she said, and tried to leave it there.

"You're going to have to do better than that," I said. "There's a lot of talk, you know."

"I don't mind the talk," she said. "Let them talk. It only shows what they don't know."

"I don't talk," I said.

"I know," Kelly said. She drew her legs up toward her and everything was silent for a few seconds. "Okay," she said. "The official reason is that I was trying to 'disseminate and distribute' drugs on campus."

"What's the difference between disseminate and distribute?"

"Right?"

"So that's the official version. What's the real version?"

"A bunch of us had decided to trip together—about fifteen of us—so I bought a sheet of acid and we were all going to take it together and help each other, but one of the girls freaked out and reported me."

"Freaked on the acid?"

"No, before that. We never even got to take it. I think what really pissed them off was that the headmaster's face was on the tabs. And I wouldn't tell them where I'd gotten the sheet. I still don't see what the big deal was, we'd been reading Michael Pollan in class. They should have kicked the girl out."

"Did the teacher get in trouble?"

"The girl's parents raised a stink, I guess, but the headmaster stood up for the teacher for once. The headmaster supposedly told the parents that the students read a lot of stuff, like about Abraham Lincoln, but that doesn't mean students will want to be John Wilkes Booth."

"That's a little badass. I don't think our principal would play it like that."

Kelly shrugged. "I still got kicked out. That's fine. It really wasn't right for me. I like getting into trouble. And getting out of it. I got out of there all right."

It was easy to talk to her, and Zeno seemed to like her. His large head rested on her feet and it was getting late. Kelly didn't seem in a rush.

"I don't think anyone's going to come," I said.

"Maybe I should have moved my car."

"Because you want them to come. I don't. Whatever keeps them away is fine with me."

"You don't want to know who it is?"

"It could be nobody," I said. "Somebody lost or whatever."

"You think so?"

"I'd like to think so. But you never know. My dad attracts a rough audience."

"From the bar?"

"From the bar," I said. I hesitated to say anything else. "A lot of shady people, a lot of shady stuff. I'll tell you about it sometime."

"I like shady stuff," Kelly said. "Hearing about it, anyway."

"I think maybe more than just hearing. That's why you came over."

"Maybe. Should I move the car?"

"You'll have to wake up Zeno."

"Then we'll leave it," she said.

Should I say more? I think I'll leave a little mystery for my father to figure out.

I flew into Mexico City and rented a car. I texted my brother that I was in the country and driving to his property. He didn't respond. I drove west for a few hours, arcing north and then west through the city, connecting with autopista 134, which took me beyond the ten million people of the city and out into the country, winding through the hills and the suburbs and then north of a large lake. I didn't know where I was going, just following the GPS and hoping there would be something at the end. I drove until there was no city, no highway, just a road that kept winding up into the hills and then through a small town I probably shouldn't name.

I couldn't see Al here, couldn't imagine him making a life for himself. That's the trouble with imagination sometimes, it has limits and blind spots. I could only think of Al back home, with me and Sara and Zeno, or back in the past somewhere, in a place that no longer exists. I could only think of him coming here if he was in trouble, or thought he was in trouble, that he wouldn't come down here because he wanted to but because he had to come. It was an escape, not a destination. I tried to think of it the other way. I thought of *All the Pretty Horses* and hoped that maybe Al could find a better life in this country and put the past behind him and maybe he'd meet a beautiful woman who would give him happiness and peace. I kept driving and hoping he would be where I thought he was. If he wasn't, then we were both in trouble.

I was a good husband. I've been a good brother, and I've been a good father. I provided for my family, which seems to be what people care most about. I loved them and respected and protected them. It's like James Baldwin said, that the only success people care about in this country is wealth. I played that game, and won, I just didn't post my score so people could see it. I had enough, more than enough, but not enough in the end, it turned out. I'd made more than I would ever need, getting my hands mildly filthy in the process, and then almost lost it all. Or had it taken, I should say.

On her way out, to go off with another man, my wife decided she'd take what she could. Wedding ring and daughter she'd leave behind, but money she'd take. As much as she could get away with. She never had to worry about money, but she worried about it anyway, and when the time came, she tried to steal it from me. I would have given her everything, so it doesn't matter how much she took, it's the fact that she took it. She could have asked for it, and she'd have gotten a lot more than what she stole. Instead, I had to hide it, protect it. I had to make sure she wouldn't get a dime more than what she took. But that was for Sara. She's got college all paid for, and then some. She doesn't ever have to worry about money, doesn't have to worry about what to study because she won't be able to pay off her loans. She can study what she wants, wherever she wants and for as long as she wants. And when she's done, she doesn't have to work if she doesn't want to. She can volunteer, take a low-paying job that satisfies her, do whatever calls to her. That's all set. I've done that. I was good to my family, and still I feel like I didn't do enough.

My wife left me, my brother wanted to kill me. I must have done something for it to happen.

I don't know why I feel the need to defend myself. You can judge for yourself. I could have told the story of me as the good husband, recounted all the things I did for my wife and recounted her betrayal. I could have told you that story. I could have told you the story of me as a good brother, and I suppose it's still part of this one, our lives so entwined with each other, but I could have concentrated solely on the story of Al's wife and her diagnosis of cancer and how we supported Al and Vera through all of the pain and devastation and Al's struggles afterward and how I helped him, started carrying him the way he'd carried me. I could have told that story; it's a sad one with maybe a happy ending. Or I could have told you Sara's story and how when my wife left, she didn't only leave me, but left Sara too, never wanted her to come with her, never invited her, never mentioned it, and, as far as I know, never had anything to do with her after she left, until recently. I could tell the story of how Sara and I were there for each other, how close we became, forging a deeper bond than I ever thought possible. And I could tell you how she's turned out to be an amazing person. I could tell that story. Instead, I'm telling this one, which maybe doesn't put me in the best light, but is as honest as I can be about everything and runs through all those stories I didn't tell, the versions of me that are also true, but then not. Because you have to know this story. The others don't mean anything without it. And I don't even know how it's going to end, but I don't want it to end in a tiny hill town in Mexico, maybe a tiny hill town anywhere.

Maybe we all think it will end differently, that fate has something else in store. No one probably thinks they're going to end up poor and lonely, lost and afraid, betrayed and beaten. No one thinks that, do they? I never gave it much thought at all, except I thought that my life would be made up of phases, and not a connected string of events. When we started loading trucks back when we were still in high school, I thought it was just a phase, that we'd pay off our debt and move on to something else, then when we started making money, I thought we'd only do that for a while and then move on. And we did move on, but not in the ways I thought, and then five years passed, and then five more, and it's almost as if each phase were a dream, time passing as you slept and when you wake up you realize that time has passed, that black almost formless notion of time when you sleep where everything can happen, but when you wake up you realize that the only thing that has happened is that the dream is over and time has been wasted and the opportunities to move on have dwindled, and the alternatives disappeared, and you start to feel trapped, or diminished. I never thought I'd stay in the same place, doing the same thing, for most of my life. I'm not complaining, just ruminating, as one does when you see a new place, new landscapes, and are reminded of everything you haven't seen. You want things to change, then you count on them staying the same, the same routine, the same steady work, the same relationships, a stability that is comforting and secure—and then change comes when you don't want it, or it's the wrong kind of change that upsets everything. I've tried to be happy, even when happiness was taken away, be satisfied with what I have and not want the things I don't have. I've tried, and still wound up unsatisfied.

I didn't know where I was going before I met Al. I didn't think about the future, I barely thought about the next day until it arrived, just tried to get through each day as it came. I had a few friends, but they were as lost as I was, a small group of teenagers drifting along as if we were never going to grow up, never going to have to look out for ourselves or make a decision of consequence. We thought that the future would somehow, miraculously, take care of itself, and we didn't have to actively participate in it. We'd get jobs, get girls, get rich, get famous, get everything we ever dreamed of, without having to do one single thing to achieve it. I don't know where I'd be if Al had never moved into town, but it wouldn't have been good. It was fate that he showed up when he did. And he not only showed up, he took over. He had it all figured out, and he not only had the plans, he knew how to put them in motion.

He wanted to make money, "and the way to make money is to take," he said. He was always looking out for something to take, something to steal so we could make some money, any money, and then we'd put that money to work. That's why he ran and stole the chips off the truck. We might have stumbled into it, but it was all part of Al's larger scheme, the same way taking over the bar was, taking over the hardware store, seeing crypto early on, seeing Mexico, all of it. Al didn't know the future—he didn't have to know it—he made it for himself, and for me too. The same was true in my marriage. I moved along in my familiar daily routine, but my wife made the big decisions. I was happy to let her take the lead on the house, take the lead with raising Sara, follow her wherever she wanted to take us. I thought she was happy about that too. I didn't want to think about it.

I looked at the countryside—it was entirely different from back home, but exactly the same. I wasn't that far from one of the biggest cities in the world, but it seemed far away from this small town with the road winding up through the hills. The traffic dwindled to nothing and the houses thinned into anomalies on the landscape. I never had to think about what was ahead; Al did that, my wife did that, it was taken care of. Now I had to make decisions.

I kept driving on the narrow two-lane road that curled and angled its way up the hill until I was in a small village of no more than a few thousand people about two thousand feet up. It was chilly, around fifty degrees, and I lowered the window and let the cool air come into the car, fresh and clean like a straight razor scraping the numbing lethargy of the flight and the drive away. I drove through the small center of town, dominated by a white church with a stone bell tower, and then back out to the two-lane road with empty fields on either side and here and there stone houses set back from the road. Mountains rose into the sky in the distance and I could see why Al wanted to buy land here, maybe build a house. I was wrong about it; I could see him in a place like this. It was like home, but entirely different. I thought that if you replaced the short, spiky trees with oaks and pines it would be just like home, but of course it wouldn't be at all. It was nothing like home. There was an emptiness to it, not just in the fields that stretched all the way to the mountains, it seemed, and in the lack of houses, but in the houses themselves, in the road and the sky and in the lonely, thin air. My reason for being there was to give Al what was his, but my thought was to take Al home. I never thought that maybe he wouldn't want to come back; I never thought I'd want to stay. I only thought we were passing through.

It was exactly like the picture Al had shown me, an empty lot, a barren patch of dirt and grass and weeds looking out over the valley. I don't know what I expected, a house with a welcome mat out front, the door open with Al waving me inside. Or maybe just Al sitting in a lawn chair on the undeveloped land he owned, waiting for me to come after him. I don't know what I expected or why I should have expected anything other than this empty lot, with no house, no chair, and no Al. Of course there was nothing.

I took a picture and sent it to Sara. Then I sent it to Al. Maybe if he knew I was there, standing in his spot, he would respond. He did not.

I went and sat in the car and waited, looking at this magnificent view of the mountains in the distance and suddenly I felt sad, the way you feel after a great loss, and the mountains seemed darker and more distant and I had no idea what I was doing there. I was tired and alone and didn't know what to do or where to go, and I closed my eyes and couldn't look at the mountains anymore and thought about Sara and Zeno. I didn't know if I had the energy to get back to them. I didn't know if I had the strength to get back on the road. I closed my eyes and tried not to think about it, tried to think about what to do next. Maybe Al wasn't here at all, but some other place, a secret place only he knew about thousands of miles from where I was right now. Maybe Mexico was nothing, just a decoy, a story he told so he could go someplace else where no one would find him. It could be that he was gone for good. I tried to think about what to do next, to solve the problem at hand. And then I woke up.

I'd only been asleep about thirty minutes. The lot was still empty, the mountains still there, and I was still there. And Al was still not there. I turned the car around and drove back into town. I thought the village looked like the one at the end of *The Treasure of the Sierra Madre*, where the gold gets blown back into the dirt. "A great joke played on us by the Lord, or Fate, or Nature." Then I remembered the bandits digging their graves and getting shot by the federales. It didn't look anything like that. There were stores and cars, no bandits or federales, no graves. And still, no stinking badges.

I drove back into the small town, past the church, and looked for a restaurant. I didn't see anything. There was a gas station, a stationery store, and then a small convenience store, a miscelánea with a faded red awning. I parked the car and walked in the open door, partially blocked by cases and cases of Coca -Cola, the red crates almost reaching the ceiling. It was a clutter of house supplies and grocery items, wallpaper rolls and ribbons, toys and pest poisons. I bought a bottle of energy drink and some candy bars and asked about a hotel. "Dónde está el hotel," I think I said. The guy behind the counter shook his head.

"Not here," he said. "Santiago del Monte."

That was more than thirty minutes away. I wasn't sure I could make it. I walked back to the car but didn't get in. I didn't know where to go. I didn't want to leave town, leave the only spot I knew was connected to Al. Maybe I could buy a tent and pitch it on Al's lot and wait for him to turn up. I leaned against the driver's door of the rental car and looked into the window of the store and ate a candy bar. I tried calling Al again. There was no answer and I didn't leave a message. I took a picture of the store and sent it to Al. "In front of this store. Not sure what to do next. You tell me. I'm asking you to tell me. Stay or go?"

I got into the car and ate another candy bar and could almost feel the sugar surging up to my brain. I'd go to the hotel in Santiago del Monte and figure things out. Give it another day or so. Before I started the engine, my phone dinged. It was a message from Al.

"Go to the hotel," he had texted.

"In Santiago del something?" I texted.

"No."

"Where?"

I could see the dots blinking on the screen as he typed his reply, and I could almost sense his exasperation with me.

"Go back into the store. Tell them you're waiting for me. They'll help you."

"Then what?"

Nothing. I tried calling him again. Nothing.

I went back into the store and showed the man a picture on my phone, an image of Al and me. "Conoces este hombre?" I asked.

He studied the image and shook his head. "I don't know that man," he said. "I don't know him."

"Mi hermano," I said and pointed to Al in the image. "Es esperando me."

He was speaking perfect English and I was still talking crap kitchen Spanish. He studied the photograph again and then looked at me with indecision. I showed him another picture. I showed him five or ten, scrolling through a bunch on my phone. "He told me to talk to you," I said. "He said you'd help me find the hotel. The hotel where he's waiting for me."

"Follow me," he said. "I'll take you."

He closed his shop and got in his car and I followed him as he drove down the hill. I didn't know where we were going, but I knew it wasn't going to be Santiago del Monte.

I picked up Kelly around four-thirty in the morning and we drove down and parked near an old warehouse. It was a big brick building that could hold a couple of football fields in it. It had been built in the thirties, I think, sometime before World War II anyhow, and they'd made brass fittings or fans or clocks or something, and when the war came they converted to shells or tanks or some other thing that was needed more than whatever they made before, and they hired anyone who was still around, mostly women. My great -grandmother worked there. We used to have a photo of her standing outside the factory, in her denim coveralls, a bandana holding back her hair. She still had her lipstick on. She looked badass. I think my mother took the picture when she left, or maybe got rid of it. She threw out a lot of stuff—photographs, papers, letters, jewelry, artwork she and my father bought together, a chair, a lamp, most of it smashed and torn and dumped in the garbage bins in the garage—all the things that reminded her of my father, I guess. "Why couldn't she just leave?" Dad said.

Anyway, the warehouse. It was one of three big factories during the war, and when the war ended, it went back to whatever it did before and fired almost all of the women and hired the men back. It still did well, until the eighties or so, when manufacturing started leaving. It sat empty for a long time. I know all of this because I did a paper on it for school. I've forgotten a lot of the details, but you get the idea. Now the trucks come in and out, making deliveries to other businesses. Sort of like a business-to-business Amazon service. They're the trucks that deliver to my father and Al, or to another guy who delivers to them. It's not always the same and I'm not a hundred percent sure of who does what, but we were there to watch the trucks, to count them, note what time they came and went, how many drivers, and maybe follow some of them. It would have been better if we'd been in separate cars, but I didn't want to sit there by myself, so I had Kelly in the car with me. It made a difference, a big difference.

I was popular at school, but Kelly was cool. She had a way about her, a casual confidence, or disregard, not arrogance but quiet assurance, that drew people to her. She also dressed better than anyone else—not with more expensive clothes, but more interesting ones, vintage stuff, secondhand stuff, brothers' hand-me-downs, that she wore in combinations no one else could pull off. There's an Italian word for it, I think, an effortless chic that draws people's attention. Girls were always asking her advice.

And she was outlaw. Her reputation preceded her, getting kicked out of school, and for drugs. There were rumors of other stuff. She knew her way around the dark web, buying all sorts of illegal stuff. Or that she got revenge on the girls at the private school, broke into their houses and trashed their rooms. There were a couple of girls whose father's got arrested, indicted, whatever, for fraud, drug trade, trafficking, serious stuff. People said Kelly had tipped off the cops. I didn't believe it. That was all just talk. Kelly didn't say anything about it. And I didn't ask her. We talked about a lot of stuff, however, and by the time she was with me in the car she knew about my dad and Al.

"You know how much money your Dad has?" she asked me.

"Enough to get me through college, that's about all he says about it. We don't really talk about it. He doesn't act like he has much; he certainly doesn't spend it. Look at my car."

"He has plenty, I bet," Kelly said. "He knows how to hide it."

"Maybe."

"Look at those guys who got arrested. They lived a large life. You can't live like that and not get noticed. Not around here. Your dad is smarter than that. Did he work with any of them?"

"No. He keeps it close. He only works with my uncle and a few other people. He stays away from all those other idiots. He doesn't like that way of life. I don't think he would live like that even if he could."

There was nothing going on at the warehouse. Not yet. We were too early. We drank our coffee and looked at the empty street and blank warehouse.

"I like the way you live," Kelly said. "We have too much. And it's still not enough."

"How much?" I was joking, not expecting an answer.

"Plenty, I think. But not enough to last. My dad made his money the old-fashioned way; he inherited it. And there's some in a trust. But that'll get split between me and my two brothers and a dozen cousins. I'm not counting on it. I don't even really think about it. You?"

"Only when I'm driving," I said.

The trucks started coming. Vans and cars, pulling into the

warehouse and then pulling out a half hour or so later. We wrote down license plate numbers, marked the arrival and departure times, took pictures, tried to gather as much information as we could. We would come back tomorrow and see what was the same and what was different. We'd come back after that if my father thought we needed to.

"Do they have the money when they come, or only when they go out?" Kelly said.

"I don't know. I honestly don't know how it works, exactly. Other than the money gets distributed out, filtered through a bunch of businesses, and then comes back clean. At least I think that's how it works."

"And your dad and uncle are part of it."

"A very small part, way down the ladder. It's barely illegal, what they do, really."

"You're like Meadow Soprano," Kelly said.

"Hardly. More like Mary Corleone."

"God, let's hope not. Doesn't she get killed?"

"Oh, yeah. That's part three. I always forget about three. I meant part two, when she's barely even in the story, almost totally ignored. That's me."

"You're not ignored," she said, and I was glad that she was there with me.

A man came out of the warehouse, nicely dressed, vaguely familiar. Familiar to me, vaguely to Kelly.

"Who's that?" she asked.

"That's ████████," I told her. "That's who my father and uncle work with."

"He's the boss."

"*A* boss anyway," I said. "I can't imagine he's running everything."

"I know him," Kelly said. "Or, I should say, I know his daughter. I went to school with her."

"What's the daughter's story?"

"Thorns on the outside, acid on the inside. You know the type. Bethany."

"I know the type. No one calls her Beth."

"No one," Kelly said. "I got along with her, though. She was one of the girls who was going to trip with us."

"But not the one who ratted on you."

"No. Bethany wanted to murder her. She might have. I don't know. I was gone by then."

"You're not in touch with Bethany?"

"Not really. I bet she'd be up for something, though. You have something in mind?"

"Maybe," I said.

After a few minutes, Bethany's dad reappeared and went back into the warehouse. Kelly jumped out of the car and hurried after him. I didn't know what she was doing and I didn't know what to do, whether to drive off and leave her there to fend for herself, or whether to rush in after her and help her if she was any trouble. Of course, she was going to be in trouble, the question was if I wanted to join her. I did not. But I didn't drive off; I stayed. In no time, Bethany's dad was escorting Kelly out of the warehouse. He didn't look pleased. Kelly was talking a mile a minute and kept smiling at him and nodding her head. "Thank you," I could hear her say as she walked away from him. "Really, thank you. I appreciate your help." He went back inside and Kelly hurried to the car.

"What was that all about?" I said.

"I told you I like getting into trouble. We can go."

I drove off and it seemed like Kelly was not going to say anything else.

"So, what happened? What did you do back there?"

"I walked right in," she said. "No one paid any attention to me, until I got to Bethany's father. He was pissed."

"He looked it," I said.

"That was nothing compared to when he first saw me, but I told him I was a friend of his daughter's and that I'd been kicked out of our school, and I told him why, or a version of it, and told him that I was hoping to be reinstated in the fall and wondered if he would help me."

"And how'd that go over?"

"You saw him bring me out. I don't care. I only needed to say something, anything, to explain why I was there and that's what popped out. He wasn't happy, but it worked. He didn't think I was there to snoop around."

"But you didn't snoop around."

"I didn't have to. They were all right there in the open. You could see them handling a bunch of money, right there. They didn't even have the door locked."

"No one probably ever does what you just did. What else?"

"Isn't that enough?" Kelly said. "They have the money, a lot of it. Right there."

"I'm not sure we need it," I said. "I'm thinking of a different angle."

"Me too," Kelly said. "There's more than one angle here."

"We could make a recommendation."

"Or two. Maybe we recommend both. I'm telling you, this looked easy."

"It's not," I said. "I guarantee it."

"You want to go higher risk, higher reward?"

"We should think it through," I said.

"I've been thinking," Kelly said. "I think we can do it."

I followed the car down the main road for a few miles, then he took a sharp turn down a dirt road, where we drove another few miles. The road was choked on each side by shrubs and small trees, thick and wild, and I thought for a minute that the guy was leading me off into the woods where he would rob me or worse. I thought about turning around, but kept following until the trees cleared and you could see a large piazza, with a hotel. It was a beautiful two-story adobe brick building with white colonnades on each level. I'd seen this hotel before. Al had shown me the rendering. The driver pointed to the entrance and waved at me, then turned around and sped off back the way we had come.

I parked and went into the lobby and waited until a guy came out like Anthony Perkins in *Psycho*, not expecting to see anyone, not wanting to see anyone.

"Hola," I said and tried to continue with "Puedo conseguir una habitacion?" It must have come out as something else.

"In English," he said.

"Can I get a room?"

"No rooms. Sorry."

"Is there another hotel nearby?"

"Not nearby, no."

"I'm looking for my brother," I said. "I thought he might be here." I took out my phone and showed him a couple of pictures of Al and me together. "Alejandro," I said. "He's my brother. I'm supposed to meet him here."

"I don't know," he said.

"You haven't seen him?"

He shook his head, but not convincingly.

"Maybe you know his father," and I told him the name. He didn't seem to like the sound of it.

"No," he said. "I don't know them."

He was lying, but I didn't know what to do. I stood there for a second, hoping he might change his mind, but he ignored me and pretended to do some work on the computer in front of him.

I went outside and called Sara. She didn't answer, so I texted her again. Then I called Al. Left a message, sent a text. "At the hotel. Not helpful. Waiting out front." No reply. Then I called our man in the office. He answered. He always does.

"We're out of pocket for a couple of days," I told him. "Al's out of the country. I'm trying to find him."

"And what's Al doing?"

"Our friends in the bars got mixed up with some people down here," I told him. "Al's trying to straighten it out."

"How bad is it?"

"It shouldn't take more than a couple of days."

"It's not going to be a problem?"

"Al knows the people down here. He'll straighten it out."

"I'm counting on it."

I didn't know what I was saying. Buying time, mostly. But I didn't have much of it. There was money in the safe and work to be done back home. The bar would be closed and the hardware store open, but not for our usual business. That had to get started again when we got back. And I didn't have a clue how long that would be. I went back to the car and sat and waited.

It was Al's hotel, the one he talked about building. It was right there in front of me, so new they hadn't finished the road to it, but it was so perfectly placed in the landscape it looked as if it had been there forever. I looked along the two rows of wooden doors, recessed back from terra-cotta walkways that looked out toward the piazza, looked for any sign of life, but the doors remained closed. I waited for almost an hour and then was thinking that maybe I should go and sit in the lobby, when a car pulled up and four men got out and an older man turned toward me and I immediately thought it was Al's father.

I watched them go up to the second floor and enter one of the rooms. I sat and waited, hoping that Al would follow, but when he didn't, I walked to the room and knocked.

One of the three younger men opened the door and looked at me. I could see the older man standing in the room. I could see Al in his face, the same hooded eyes that displayed caution and seriousness, with none of the light Al had. It was a face that could hold a grudge, put it there in front of him so you would know what was between you.

"I'm looking for Alejandro," I said.

The man shook his head and was beginning to close the door, when the older man told me to come in. I entered the room and the door closed behind me, and I wasn't sure I'd made the right choice. I wasn't sure I was going to get back out of the room alive.

The three younger men eyed me with suspicion, a threatening wariness. They were the father's protection, I figured, and most certainly armed. I was nothing more than a target, a bright bullseye that had bumbled into their room. I tried my best to ignore them and looked directly at Al's father.

"I'm Al's brother," I said. "I'm Mary Carver's son."

He pulled his mouth down at the corner in an expression that acknowledged what I had said and dismissed it at the same time.

"These are my sons," he said, motioning to the men next to him. They still looked like hired security to me. I looked more like Al's father than these guys. "Mary Carver. That was a long time ago. She was trouble. And how about her son, what kind of trouble are you bringing?"

"No trouble," I said. "I'm looking for Alejandro."

"And you think he's with me?"

I didn't know what to say. Maybe Al didn't want me to meet his father, maybe he didn't even know he was here. Maybe I'd already said too much, said something I shouldn't have.

"No," I said. "But I've seen this hotel before. He showed me a picture once. I thought I'd see his place for myself."

"This is not his place," he said. "This is not his. It was a dream for him, but only a dream. This is mine. I made this happen."

"I'm sure that would make Alejandro happy," I said. "That's why I came down here. To try and make him happy. Maybe you've already done that."

"I would like to make my son happy," he said. "Do you think it's possible?"

"I'd like to think so," I said.

He got up out of his chair and left the room with one of his men. The other two stood in the corner like lamps. Lamps with guns.

I stood and watched them for a minute. But before they turned me into another lamp, I texted Al again. Then I texted Sara a picture I'd taken of the front of the hotel. I put my phone back in my pocket. Al's father and his shadow came back into the room.

"Maybe all he needs is a fresh start," he said, picking up on our conversation as if he had never interrupted it. "Build his house, stay here with me. What do you think about that?"

"That's for him to decide," I said.

"There's a description in *The Beautiful and Damned* that reminds me of Alejandro," he said. "Have you read it?"

I shook my head. "Only *Gatsby*," I said.

"You should read more Fitzgerald. 'If you want to learn about America, read Fitzgerald,' somebody said. Do you know who?"

I shook my head again.

"'If you want to learn about Spain, read Hemingway; if you want to learn about America, read Fitzgerald.' You don't know who said that? They were wrong about Hemingway. Maybe they're wrong about Fitzgerald. What do you think?"

"Everybody's wrong about everything, aren't they?" I said, and he looked at me the way you look at a fly on the wall that you're determined to smash. Then he smiled, which only made it worse.

"Anyway, what did I want to tell you? The description. Fitzgerald writes that the main character, that he was 'wedded to a melancholy for the rest of his life,' which perfectly describes Alejandro, doesn't it, ever since Vera, I mean."

"He's better now," I said. "I see it. The old Al is coming back."

"I'd like to see a new version, not the old," he said. "Anyway, he knows you're here. He'll be here in a while. I'll get you something to eat and drink and we can wait for him."

"I'll wait for him downstairs," I said and started to leave.

"Maybe we can talk while we wait," he said. "You can tell me how Sara is doing."

I stopped and turned back toward him. He must have seen the surprise on my face. "You think I don't know everything about you? You think Al hasn't told me? And what do you know about me?"

"I know you have me at a disadvantage," I said. "I don't know much at all about you. Al keeps his own counsel about you."

"I didn't recognize you," he said. "It's been a while since I've seen your picture. Alejandro said some people might come looking for him, so I was cautious. You have to be cautious. There aren't too many people who know where he is, where he might be, and not too many people know about this place."

"It looks that way."

"It looks that way," he said. With sarcasm. "Every room here is booked. Booked every night for nine months. Every room is empty. But every room is booked. You understand?"

"I understand."

"Not so different from a bar or from a hardware store. Am I right?"

"A lot different," I said. "The bar is a bar, some alcohol, some food, a few regulars; the hardware store is a place where people come for a hammer, a rake, maybe a flyswatter, some rat poison. This place is magnificent. It really is."

"This place is, like you said, a dream. But this place is for family. You understand?"

"I understand."

"You don't," he said. "Not really. But you will."

Al's father had gone from reticent to effusive, sitting next to me, almost hovering over me, making sure I liked the food he'd ordered, asking if I wanted anything else, and talking nonstop, a constant stream of information about the famous architect who designed the hotel, the famous designers who outfitted it, the famous people who had stayed there (or, more important, wanted to stay there but were turned away), the famous bands who had played in the ballroom, and he talked about my childhood. He said that he had met me a few times.

I didn't remember. I didn't know if any of it was true. He said that he remembered me well, that he was impressed by me, and that he wanted for me and Al to know each other.

"Your mother didn't want it," he said, "but especially your grandmother. She didn't want it at all. She didn't want me around. I don't blame her, but she deprived you of a friend, of a brother, of a better childhood. Your grandmother did that."

"And my mother."

"She would have listened to me. There was a time when she would have listened."

"I never knew her that way."

"It wasn't a long time," he said and smiled and moved his chair closer, as if everything he was telling me was only between the two of us. The three other men who were sitting across the room were ignored for now.

"We all could have been under one roof," he said. "But we can still make it happen. We can do that here."

"I have to get back to Sara," I said. "And work."

"There is nothing you do there that you can't do here," he said. "And Sara? Sara would love it here. She should come here. We should make that happen."

"Maybe after she graduates," I said.

He shook his head. "She needs to come here soon. The family needs to be together."

And then the door opened and Al came in. I was finishing my steak and he did not look particularly happy to see me, and honestly, I wasn't entirely happy to see him. He looked at me suspiciously and I probably looked back at him in the same way. His father jumped up and grabbed Al and led him to me.

"This is a good day," the father said. "We are here together. We should do something special."

"You should move your car," Al said to me.

"One of the boys can do that," Al's father said and held out his hand for the keys.

"I brought you something," I said to Al. "It's in the car."

"Let's go get it," Al said, and we walked down to the rental.

"What's going on?" I said.

"You tell me."

"I came to bring you home."

"I thought you said you had something for me."

"I do," I said and opened the trunk of the car. I reached into my bag and brought out Al's external drive.

"Take this and let's get out of here," I said and handed him his drive.

"It doesn't change anything."

"It changes everything. Isn't this what the fuss is all about? Take it."

Al took it and then tossed it back in the trunk.

"It's useless," he said.

"What do you mean?"

"There's nothing on it," Al said.

"There's nothing on it? Then why did we go all the way to California?"

"Because it's mine," he said. "And somebody took it. Even if it's nothing, it's my nothing and I wanted it back."

I didn't believe him. He could see it on my face. I don't think he cared.

"I know what you're thinking," he said. "And what Sara thought was on it, it's not. You understand?"

"I thought you said there was seven million dollars on it."

"Not now. I have maybe a couple million total to my name."

"That's not nothing. That's a lot of money."

"Then that's why we went to California. Jesus, Peck. I don't know what to tell you. Two million is a lot of money, but not for the rest of my life. It'll last me twenty years, maybe, till I'm sixty-five, if I'm lucky. And

I intend to be around past sixty-five, so I'm going to need a lot more than that. And some of it in a hurry."

"You've still got the hardware store."

"I don't," Al said. "I had to sign it over to Fitz."

"What?"

"He was bleeding me, Peck. And what he didn't take, that asshole at Bishop's Corner took."

"Those problems are gone. We can get back to work."

"It's not safe there," he said.

"It's safe, Al. Everything's going to be fine. Come back and things will be better. There's still a life for you there, a better life. Is there a life for you here?"

"My father thinks so."

"Do you believe him?"

Al didn't say anything.

"Should we believe him? Is any of this real? Are those even his sons?' I asked him.

Al laughed a little. "Yes? No? Maybe? I don't know. I don't even know if those are the same guys I met last time I was down here. He's mostly talk, I know that much."

"How do you handle it?"

"I don't believe anything he says, but I accept everything he tells me," Al said.

"And how's that worked out?"

"I'm broke," he said.

"You're not broke."

"I need money," he said. "My father will get me work. I need to stay down here, Peck."

"I need you back home."

"I can't go back there. I can't afford it. I need money. And fast."

"We've spent our whole lives worrying about money. The vast majority of it wasn't even ours, but we worried about it anyway. Don't you want to stop thinking about money?"

"It's easy when you have it," Al said.

"Whatever I have is yours."

"I can't do that," he said. "And I can't go back. I'm tired of it. Tired of being stuck in the same small town, working the same way we did when we were young, answering to somebody else instead of ourselves, and for what?"

"You had your eyes open," I said. "You sound like you didn't make anything in the bargain."

"What I had was taken from me," Al said. "And I'm going to get it back. That's why I'm here." His father was a con man, maybe a good one. I didn't know. He'd taken a lot of money from Al, but he was an easy mark in this one instance. I suspected that Al would keep giving his father money, even though he said otherwise.

"We'll figure it out. But come back. You can sell your house, come live with me and Sara. I'll give you money. We'll figure it out. I need you. Sara needs you. Zeno needs you. I can't do it without you, Al. None of it. You have to come back."

"I can't. You know I can't. At least, not right now. Besides, my father has to make things right," he said.

"Okay. But don't ask him for money," I said. "Ask him for a favor."

"What do you mean?"

I wasn't quite sure. It was half an idea, maybe not even that much, but I thought that maybe Al's father could help us, help Al get out of the jam back home. But could he? I had no idea, not when I proposed it to Al. I needed the old Al to think about it, to figure out the plan, focus on the details, and get us to the finish.

I called and told him that Al had sorted it all out. "Fitz and Bishop were going after your end," I told him. "They were using a cartel down here to take it from you."

"That's not my understanding," he said.

"Yeah, they probably only told you that they were getting rid of me and Al. They didn't tell you the bigger plan. Why would they? And think about it, what would they really have to gain by getting rid of Al and me? You see the bigger picture here."

"And how does Al know all this?"

"Al's father is down here. He seems to know what's going on. Do you know who"—I gave him the name of a well-known cartel leader—"is?"

"That's his father?"

"Worked for him. Some construction work or something. HVAC jobs, I think. It doesn't matter. He knows the guy. Al hasn't been in touch with him for years, but they've reconnected recently and when this got put into motion, he reached out to Al."

"You think the father had something to do with this?"

"Not that way. This got started by Fitz. That's absolutely clear. Fitz approached them, owed them money and was looking to move up and wanted to get me and Al out of the way. Al's father reached out to Al when he heard about it. And when it came back on Fitz, Al got it to stop there. It could have escalated. The cartel wanted more. They still do. Fitz laid it out for them, got you in a tangle of trouble. Al's trying to untangle it. There's a settlement to be had here, I think."

He was quiet for a long time, long enough for me to think that I'd run out of lies to tell him and wasn't sure I could make up any more details. Luckily, he came back with a question I'd already figured out the answer.

"What do they want?"

"Ten percent," I said. "They'll take the ten and leave us alone."

"That's not leaving us alone," he said. "That's them living with their hands in my pockets. That's not a settlement, that's a down payment on a takeover. Ten percent. Not a chance."

"It could have been a hundred," I said.

"You'd take the ten."

"I don't like the idea myself, but I don't know what else to offer. I hope you can see another way around it," I said.

"I'll let you know," he said.

Al's father had a private jet. I don't know if it was his, if he rented a share, or if he had just conned his way onto one. It was hard to tell with him. He was slantwise with everything, with his words, his hotel, his security detail, even his son. I didn't trust him as far as I could throw a Cessna Citation, but we needed him. I flew back with the father and his security sons and duffel bags filled with enough assault rifles to scare the NRA. There wasn't supposed to be any violence, but you don't bring that much hardware and ammunition for nothing. It made me nervous; I couldn't stop glancing over at the black duffels, as if they were filled with live animals that might escape at any moment. The security sons drank and ate and joked and slept and ignored me. Al's father was in the cockpit. Al stayed at the hotel. It was better that way. If there was going to be violence, I didn't want him anywhere nearby. I wasn't sure if half a continent would be enough distance between him and what might happen.

I watched the duffel bags and couldn't help but think of Chekhov. When one of the sons looked at me, I asked him, "Do you know about Anton Chekhov and the gun?"

"No hagas promesas que no puedas cumplir," he said.

I only understood one word of that. Promesas. I nodded at him and tried not to think about it. They could speak English—I heard them talking to Al in English—but they only spoke to me in Spanish. I didn't try to speak any more Spanish, or even English, and tried to keep my mouth shut. My thoughts drifted around, trying to remember the little Chekhov I'd read. Instead, I remembered that Hemingway didn't like Chekhov. He liked guns, though. He supposedly could handle a pistol by age four, and had an air rifle when he was five. His grandfather gave him a shotgun when he turned ten. Hemingway had a lifetime of guns, pistols and rifles and shotguns and even machine guns, and when the time came, he used his favorite, a W. & C. Scott & Son side-by-side shotgun, to blow his brains out. His wife took it to a local welder to smash it and cut it up with an acetylene torch. They buried the burned and damaged pieces in a field. Hemingway might have disliked Chekhov, but he ended his life according to Chekhov's principle.

I had a lot of time by myself on the plane. I texted Sara, I texted Al, I tried to sleep. When Al's father came back and joined us for a few minutes I tried my Chekhov line on him. "All of my sons have been to college," he said. "Medical school, chemical engineering, computer science. They are smart boys."

I reminded him that Al had not been to college.

"We'll get him there," he said. "Then he'll know as much about everything as you think you do. And what about Sara? Where does she want to go to school?"

"She's only a junior," I said. "She still has time to figure it out."

"Well, let me know. I have a lot of contacts in the admissions offices. At the best schools in the country."

I thought I could have named any college or university and he would have claimed to have a connection. I got the impression that I could have mentioned anything, and he'd claim a connection. He had everything covered, nicely spackled over with a steady stream of talk. That's what he was counting on.

"Al never had kids," he continued. "Why is that?"

"I don't know. His wife got sick before they could."

"No. That was later. They had plenty of time. He should have had kids. This is why we do this, right? For the children, and for their children. I have nine grandchildren. Six girls and three boys. The girls will take over the world. You know this. Sara. She will take over and then her daughters. I have to wait. But the granddaughters will take over. They will make things better, the way we couldn't. The women will save us from ourselves."

"We've left them a lot of problems," I said.

"And we've left them the solutions. You'll see. I'm not worried. You'll see."

I couldn't see it. Maybe Sara could, or would. All I could see were the duffel bags. That wasn't the solution. But there they were. He reached into the pocket of his jacket and pulled out a small paperback and handed it to me. I thought it was a joke. *The Secret World of Kidnapping, Hostages and Ransom*. It wasn't a joke.

"You'll see how it's done," he said. "There are ways. Solutions. You'll see. Don't worry." He returned to the cabin, the polished wood door opening and closing, separating me from the controls. That's how I took it. I looked at the paperback and then over at the security sons; they were all lost in their phones, not paying any attention to me. There was nothing to do but read and wait.

A windowless van waited for the plane when we landed. I went to my car and left the rest of them to do whatever they were going to do. At least three of them had been to college, they could figure it out without me. I didn't want to know about it. All I knew was that they were staying at a hotel near the office where the meeting was going to take place. I wasn't going to be around for any of it. That was the plan and I was happy about it.

I called Sara and told her that we'd landed.

"Am I going to get to meet Al's dad?"

"Some other time," I said.

"What's he like?"

"I'm not entirely sure," I said. "I don't trust him, that I know."

"Does Al?"

"Too much."

"Well, we have to trust him a little," Sara said. "We have to."

Al called when it was over.

"How'd it go?"

"He turned it down, just like you thought," Al said.

"You talk to him?"

"Yeah. I told him that my father freelanced. That the deal he talked about in the room wasn't what we'd worked out before."

"How'd he take it?"

"Not well. He's going to call you."

"I'm sure he will."

"You ready?"

"I'm ready. I'll call you when it's done."

████████ called almost as I finished with Al.

"How'd it go?" I said.

"Not the way you said it would."

"And why's that?"

He laid out the details. Al's father presented himself as Emilio ████████ of the ████. ████████ was not impressed. He replayed the conversation, even threw in a dumb accent for Al's father:

"You're a long way from home, Emilio. I'm not sure I can help you."

"I'm closer to home than you think. In fact, I'm buying a house near here right now, so I can be closer to my business."

"What business is that?"

"The bars and the hardware store. I own those."

"I don't know anything about that. That's between you and the owners; it's got nothing to do with me."

"They approached me on your behalf. They represented you, they said. And now they're gone. Heart attacks, they tell me. I don't know. All I know is that they owed me, so now you should take care of their debts."

"I'm willing to work with you on that, but not with the businesses. That's not what I was told would be the agreement."

"We've changed our minds. We want the businesses, and fifteen percent."

"I can't do that. I can't agree to that."

"Emilio" got up to leave. "I'll take that back to my boss. He won't be pleased."

"We could work this out between us, like adults."

"There are no adults where money is concerned," Emilio said.

That's the version I was told, not the same version that Al related, but close enough.

"That wasn't the deal," I told him.

"Apparently it's the deal now."

"What do you want to do?"

"I want to get Emilio back in the room. Can you make that happen?"

"We can try," I said.

"Trying is how we got here," he said. "I don't want any more trying. I want it done."

"We're doing what we can with a bad hand we inherited. If I'd known Fitz and Bishop were in with these guys earlier, maybe we could have made things happen differently, but Al and I are cleaning up a bad mess as best as we can. If you have a different idea, you let me know."

I'd never talked like that with him, ever. I wasn't sure how it would go over.

"All of this is new to me," he said.

"Maybe you shouldn't listen to me, take it up the ladder, see what they say."

"No. We have to put a stop to it here. But I can't take the deal they've got on the table. Understood? Get them back to what Al negotiated."

"I'll let you know. That's the best I can tell you."

I called Al back and told him what had happened.

"My father says he threatened him, just a little, and he caved. Quick."

"I'm surprised he didn't take the deal, then," I said.

"Pops would have raised him."

"He wants you to bring him back down."

"Tell him to give me a couple more days."

I told him. He wasn't happy.

"Maybe it'll be done before then," I said. "But let Al work on it. He'll get what's best for you."

"Sooner rather than later. Everything can change in a couple of days."

He wasn't wrong about that.

After school I went for a drive with Kelly. "Let's take your car," I said. She smelled like lavender and lime, calming and fresh at the same time. She sat and waited for the engine to warm up, resting her hands on the steering wheel. I noticed the tattoo on her right hand. I'd glimpsed it before, but now I had a good look at it. It was an ornate *J* that curled from her thumb, around the webbed flesh between the thumb and index finger, and ended at the base of her first finger. It was medieval, like something you'd see in an old manuscript, and it was the initial of her dead brother. I reached out with my left hand and traced the *J*. She didn't move her hand away, didn't even flinch. "My uncle has a *V* on his right wrist," I told her. "For his wife. She died from cancer five years ago." Al's tattoo went a third of the way up his wrist, with the top of the *V* touching each side of his wrist at the base of his hand. It was plain and hard and simple and I thought it was the most beautiful thing, but couldn't imagine having it there all the time, a constant reminder, constant, but I guess that was the point. "My brother had it too," she said. "Cancer. When he was ten." Kelly looked at the tattoo often, mostly just a quick glance. I hope it comforted her, gave her back a little part of what she'd lost.

"My uncle seems sad all the time," I told Kelly. "My father too.

It weighs them down, you know, like a weight they have to carry. But they carry it. And they try to keep it from me. But they carry it all the time."

"They don't have a choice," Kelly said. She took her hands off the steering wheel and I thought she was going to turn toward me but she didn't. She looked the other way. "This is what I know about it, and I'm not saying it's true for everybody, but it is for me. It's like a shadow. Some days it's long and dark and you see it all the time, all of it, the darkness of it and the weight of it. And then some days it's short, like when the sun is directly overhead and you hardly see it at all, you don't even notice it, but it's always there, and it always has that weight."

"That makes sense," I said.

"You can have happiness, like in the moment," Kelly said and turned and looked at me, "but you're never happy. Does that make sense?"

"I see it like that for my dad, but especially for my uncle. With my dad, it was betrayal, you know. His wife cheated on him, stole from him, and he's glad that she's gone, but he's not happy. And my uncle, well, you understand that."

"My parents will never be the same," Kelly said. "But you have to go on. Sometimes I don't know why or how, but you go on. You know that. You carry it too."

I didn't know what to say. Could she see it? Of course Kelly could, but could everyone, the way they see it in my dad and Al? Besides, I didn't think of myself as sad. I never did. Angry and bitter and lonely sometimes, but rarely sad. But maybe I was. I didn't want to think about it. I'm my father's daughter in that way.

We lapsed into silence and waited until the silence filled the car and started to press in on me and I had to say something to get it to stop suffocating me.

"You sure you want to do this?" I asked.

"I'm sure."

"They're going to blame you, you know."

"They'd probably blame me anyway."

Kelly picked me up early and we went and got coffee.

"Should we get one for Beth?" I said.

"Do not call her that to her face," Kelly said. "She's very sensitive about her name." Kelly ordered another coffee.

"What else is she sensitive about?"

"Everything, as far as I can tell."

"Sounds like fun."

"Are we here to have fun?"

"If we can have it," I said.

We waited for the coffees. We had the first appointments at the nail salon. Kelly had told Bethany that we'd see how it worked out, maybe make a day of it, the three of us. The coffees came and we carried them to the car.

"Anything else I should know?" I said.

"Bethany's all right. Better than most at the school, anyway. We got along, which is more than I can say for a lot of the others."

"You all right?"

"I'm all right. How about you?"

"We'll see."

We drove to the small strip mall and waited for Bethany to arrive. When Kelly saw her drive up, we got out of the car and met her and I handed her a coffee. She didn't thank me. We walked to the nail salon. We were the first customers there and we took three chairs near the back. Bethany took a seat and Kelly and I sat on either side of her. I didn't like her from the get-go. She had the annoying entitlement you find in rich kids. When we went inside, all the girls were happy to see us; they asked about my uncle and treated us like friends. Bethany didn't want to be their friend, she wanted them all to be her servants. She was curt and dismissive, and I could tell that she thought less of me that I treated them with fondness and affection. I didn't care; I wasn't going to be someone I wasn't. And maybe Bethany felt the same way. She was happy to be with Kelly, but she had no interest in me. I get along with a lot of people, most people, in fact, but Bethany rebuffed all my charms. I fished around with weak, embarrassing bait.

"My dad works with your dad," I said, and Kelly shot me a "whatareyoudoing?" look. I had to shoot her a quick "I don't know" look back.

"My dad works with a lot of people," Bethany said.

"We're not talking about families," Kelly said. "Not today. We're not talking about personal history, school, work, or anything else depressing."

"How about sex?" Bethany said.

"Only if it's good sex," I said, which at least got a laugh.

I relaxed a little and tried to concentrate on getting my toes taken care of. Kelly picked a ruby-red polish, Now Museum, Now You Don't, and Bethany picked a blue called Hide and Go Chic, and I chose Got Myself into a Jam-Balaya solely for the name. Bethany and Kelly drifted off into a conversation of their own and I stopped paying attention. I kept glancing toward the parking lot and tried to force myself not to look that way. There was the white noise chatter of conversations and I tried to hear it only as noise, without words, just the pure sound of people interacting with each other. I closed my eyes and tried to let it wash over me, a safe cloud of sound, friendly and calm. The parking lot was far away, Bethany was far away. Got Myself into a Jam-Balaya was far away. I didn't want to get out of that safe, calm moment, but it wasn't why we were there. We had been moving toward something, and ignoring it wasn't going to stop it from happening. It was too late for that.

We put on our flip-flops and stepped outside the salon. The wind was cool on my freshly painted toes. I looked quickly at the parking lot. The lot was about half full of cars, but no one was walking around. It was quiet, like a movie set after the cast and crew is gone.

"We could walk over and get some pizza," I said, nodding toward the restaurant near the end of the small strip mall.

"It's too early for pizza," Bethany said.

"They have other stuff," I said in weak protest, but Kelly had already moved on.

"I have some edibles at my house, we could go over there. No one's home."

"Let's do that," Bethany said.

We walked toward our cars, the sound of our flip-flops flapping against the asphalt making us sound like a gaggle of deranged ducks. I glanced again through the parked cars and still couldn't see it, couldn't see the future that was waiting there, patiently and with purpose. We were close to our respective cars and I glanced down and said, "I think I smudged my toe," and Bethany and Kelly stopped and looked down at my feet. Then a van appeared next to us, quietly and suddenly as if emerging out of a fog. The side door swung open just as the van stopped, and three or four men hopped out and grabbed us.

There was a bag over my head before I could see anything, before I even knew what was happening, and I was dragged and pushed into the van, with bodies bouncing into me, probably Bethany and Kelly, all of us shoved into the van as it was pulling away. Then a voice from the front yelled, "Not her, not her," and the van stopped suddenly. I could hear the door open and the same voice said, "Just those two," and I remember hoping they meant Kelly and me, but I knew that whatever was happening wasn't going to happen like that, and I remember feeling woozy, unsteady, my mind suddenly fogged and fuzzy. Then I remember hearing Kelly's voice saying, "No. Sara. Let me stay with Sara," and the sound of the van door closing, and I remember falling forward, and that's the last thing I remember.

The next thing I knew I was on an airplane with a bag over my head.

I wasn't there when it happened. I went to the market near the hardware store and got coffee and egg sandwiches and then went to Al's office. I heard Terry open the door and get ready to open for business. I went out and greeted her and she asked about Al and I told her he was still away. I asked her if she had anything she needed me to help with, but she shook her head and I went back to the office and waited. When I got tired of waiting, I went back out into the store. Dale Avery was spending too much time looking at grass seed or herbicides or something. He was a bornandbred, worked as an in-house electrician at one of the factories up the road almost as soon as he could drive a car and retired a few years ago after more than fifty years at the same job. He was usually the first customer of the day, and spent more time looking than buying, or angling to get a cup of coffee out of Al. Al was usually more than willing to buy. Now Dale was standing there, eyeing nothing in particular. Terry talked to him, asked him if he needed anything. Dale never needed anything, just a local fulfilling his daily routine. I couldn't talk to him. I was trying my best to think of it as a normal day. I was in the back counting out money to deliver later. The world moves in the same direction, day after day, the gears clicking into the usual places, right up until it all breaks down. My phone ringing was the sound of the machine breaking.

"They hit the warehouse," ████████ said.

"Who did?" I said.

"I think you know. They hit it hard. Hard."

"What do you want to do?"

"You'd better get over here. And hang on to your end."

"I'll be right there." I left the money in the safe and called Al and told him.

"They get everything?"

"Everything except ours, I think."

Al didn't say anything.

"I'm worried," I said.

"I know," he said. "I can't come back."

"I'm not asking," I said. "You need to stay there. Still, I'm worried. Maybe I should be there."

"It's not going to work that way," Al said. "You need to be there. And you need to get going."

"You're right," I said. "Thanks."

I took my coffee and drove to the city, all the time trying to not think about why I'd been summoned. But I was glad I had.

I'd thought about what to say on the way over. I would walk in and make a proposal and see what happened from there. The only trick was to come up with a solution, to not escalate things, to deal with what had happened and deal only with that. It wasn't a time to get ahead of ourselves, all that crisis management malarkey. I had to offer him something, and it had to knock him back on his heels a little. I was almost halfway there and I still didn't have anything, nothing that would make him listen, nothing that would demonstrate that I was the right guy for him to call. The right guy was Al, of course. I just hope Al knew better than to answer.

By the time I'd reached the parking garage, I still didn't have it worked out. It was the simple outline of an idea, that was all, not even anything I could really articulate. I went in like usual, waving at the security guards and acting like it was any other time, but my brain was spinning on itself, racing through options like a rat in a maze frantically trying to find its way. By the time I was on the elevator, I thought I had something, but the details eluded me. By the time I had my hand on the door to the office, the only thing I really had was the thought to keep talking, keep talking like Al's dad.

"This is what we should do," I said, and launched into a long monologue, recapping what had already happened while I frantically tried to figure something out.

"What are you proposing?" ████████ said, cutting me off.

"We don't do anything," I said. "We let them keep the money. That's what they get, and it's all they get. No businesses, no fifteen percent, none of it. They get what they took and not a penny more. That's it. We don't have to do anything else. It's that simple."

"Maybe you shouldn't be negotiating this, Peck. You have a reputation for courtesy."

"You make it sound worse than it is. I've done all right by you."

"Sometimes all right isn't enough."

"Then I wasted your time," I said. "Maybe give Al a call. Let him handle it."

"I can't reach him."

"I'll tell you what he'd say. He'd say you should hit back and hit back harder than they hit you. That's what he'd say and that's what you want to hear. But it's not what you should do. They want you to escalate this. This is how they play it. This is what they know and they know it a lot better than we do. We're not soldiers; we're businessmen. We have to take control of this in the way we know and make them play it by our rules. How much did they get? A week's worth of cash flow? Let them have it. It's the last they'll get. We'll make sure of that."

"I don't know," he said.

"You don't have to, not today, anyway. Secure the warehouse, or move everything out. We'll figure out a better system. But not today. Wait for them to make another offer."

"You don't think they'll make another move?"

"They hit the warehouse, what else are they going to take?"

I could feel us moving through space. I was sitting in a comfortable, probably leather, seat. I knew I wasn't on a commercial flight, especially with a dark hood over my head. My arms and hands weren't restrained, so I reached up and took the dark cloth off. I was sitting in a private jet, my first time, and not of my own will. There were four leather armchairs, two facing two, and three of them were occupied. Bethany was sitting directly across from me, facing me, except her face was covered with another dark hood, and her wrists were zip-tied to the armrest of her seat. There was a man sitting across the aisle from her with a gun in his lap. He looked at me and put his index finger to his lips. I pointed to Bethany and then pointed to my ear, hoping he'd understand what I was asking. He nodded and I put my hood back on.

"Can you hear me?" I said in a low voice. She didn't answer, so I assumed she couldn't. "Beth, can you hear me?" I said a little louder.

"Yes," she said at louder than normal volume.

I reminded her who I was. "They grabbed us in the parking lot. Remember?"

"Where's Kelly?"

"I don't know. I don't think she's here. I think they let her out. I heard them let her out. She was asking for you? Do you remember that?"

"No. Where are they taking us?"

"I don't know. I don't even know where we are right now."

"In a car somewhere, I guess."

I almost laughed. I took my hood off and nodded at the guy sitting next to Bethany.

"Silencio," he ordered and banged his open palm against the side of his seat for effect.

"Don't worry," I stage-whispered to Bethany. "I'm here with you."

Another man came from the back of the plane and sat in the chair next to me. He was holding a bottle of water, and when he saw me look at it, he handed it to me. And he put his index finger to his lips too. I stayed quiet.

I recognized him. He'd been in the parking lot. I think he was the one who'd grabbed me. I thought there'd been three of them, at least. Maybe the others were somewhere else on the plane, maybe they were flying it for all I knew. I only remember them grabbing us and then everything else is a blank until the plane. I didn't hurt; I wasn't sore. Maybe they'd drugged us. I wondered how they got us onto the plane, maybe carried us on in sacks, like pounds of laundry. I don't think they give a shit on those private planes. There's almost no security. No waiting around in line, no taking off your shoes and emptying your pockets, no examination of your lipstick and lotions and whatever else. Cars drive up right next to the plane and passengers get on board and take off. That's what money gets you. And that's why we were there.

I pointed to Beth's hood and pantomimed that they take it off of her. One of guards nodded and the men put on balaclavas and then took off Beth's hood. She looked at the men, then looked around at the interior of the plane, and then looked at me.

"My father's going to kill them," Bethany said. She irritated me. Immediately.

"They can understand English," I said. "So be careful what you say, or we'll both get killed."

One of the men raised his gun for effect, the other took a roll of duct tape from a pocket on his military -style pants and tore off a strip. Then he took a phone from his pocket and held it to Beth's face and took a pic of her. Then he took another phone—my phone—and held it to my face to unlock it and took my picture. He put the phones back into the pocket of his military-style jacket, and a few moments later we could hear them pinging with incoming messages. He ignored the noises for a while, then took the phones out of his pocket and turned them off and returned them to his pocket.

"I bet they sent them to our dads," I said. "All they want is money."

"They don't know what trouble they're making for themselves," Beth said. I couldn't let it go.

"You ever heard of Miroslava Breach Velducea, or Sheila Garcia and Yessenia Mollinedo?"

"No," she said.

"They were murdered by the Mexican cartels. Garcia and Mollinedo were getting out of their car to go shopping. Shot in broad daylight. They kill people all the time. And kidnap. Like, more than thirty people a day."

"How do you know so much about it?"

"Because I fucking pay attention," I said. "Because of what

our fathers do. Because of the way the world works. All these guys want is money, but if they don't get it . . ."

"My father won't pay."

"Mine will. But I don't think that will get me out. I think this is a package deal. In the meantime, don't say or do anything that will piss off these guys."

Beth looked at one of the masked men and said, "Fuck them."

The man got up and slapped the strip of duct tape over Beth's mouth in what seemed like a single, fluid motion. He then forcibly put Beth's hood back on, like someone swatting a fly with a pillow case. I sat and watched the men and thought about how this was going to play out. If Beth was telling the truth, it would be up to my father to get him to pay. We hadn't figured for any other outcome.

I was on my way home when I got the second call. was screaming now. The money was one thing, but this was different. I let him scream, and when he stopped, I told him.

"They have Sara too," I said, calmly. "And maybe Al. I don't know. I can't get ahold of him. Can you?"

He hadn't tried.

"Did you get a text with the picture?" I asked him.

"Yes."

"What does it say? Read it to me."

"'We have Bethany. She is safe. She is with us. We do not want to hurt her. We want to return her to you fast. We want an exchange.'"

"That's the same message I got," I said. "All they want is more money. That's all they want. They're not going to do anything to the girls. All they want is money. We can work with them to get the girls back."

"And how about the third girl? What happened to her?"

"They let her go," I said. "Luckily she called me before she called the cops. I told her that we'd take care of it, that all they want is money."

"I want a lot more than that," he said. "I want retaliation and punishment and pain. I want the names of the men who put their fucking hands on my daughter; I want the names of their wives and girlfriends and children; I want to know where they live; and I want their heads on a platter. And I want to be the one they see when their throats are cut. I will tear the earth off its hinges until I find them and kill them with my own hands. Isn't that what you want?"

"I promise you, the people responsible for this will be destroyed," I said. "I will take them down with my own hands. But that's for later. Let's concentrate on getting the girls back safe, and quickly, then we'll figure out the rest."

"And where's Al in all this? Wasn't he supposed to have it all figured out?"

"I don't know where he is. They've made a big play. I can't imagine they don't have Al locked down. I hope that's it. I hope that's all. I need to figure out how to get our girls back. It's going to take money."

"Get her back, Peck."

I tried to call Al, but he didn't answer. I texted him. "You ok?" About an hour later he sent me a thumbs -up emoji. That was it. "This is really bad. We need to get the girls home ASAP."

"On it," he texted back.

The plane was going down, I could feel it. There was no announcement, no "Ladies and gentlemen, we have started our descent. Please make sure your seat backs and tray tables are in their full upright position," just the gentle pull of gravity bringing us closer to the ground. One of the men got up and injected something into Bethany's arm. Another sedative. They let me stay awake and I watched as we lowered out of the clouds and down into a sprawling sea of lights, bright rivers of lights with white tributaries stretching for miles. I'd never seen so many lights; they seemed to cover everything. Bethany wouldn't see any of it.

When we landed, they carried Bethany down the few stairs to the tarmac and put her in a wheelchair and literally wheeled her a few feet to a waiting SUV. I walked, with two men right behind me; their guns were gone, or at least put away and close enough if needed. They ushered me into the SUV with Bethany slumped in the back. Her flip -flops had fallen off, and her bare feet seemed bright from the lights inside the car and I couldn't help but notice how nice her Hide-and-Go-Chic toes looked.

We were in the car for more than two hours, leaving the lights of the city behind and driving into the dark countryside, along small highways to even smaller roads, from a steady stream of oncoming lights to nothing but darkness and our headlights clearing a path. No one said anything. There was still a hood over Bethany's head and her hands were zip-tied in front of her. I held her hand, hoping she would be comforted by it when she came around.

No one spoke in the car and there was no sound except for the low hum of the tires on the road. There was nothing to see but the cone of illuminated road in front of us and I closed my eyes. Bethany's hand was warm and soft, gently oblivious like the rest of her, and before long, I was asleep next to her.

I woke up as the sound changed from the hum of pavement to the chunky thumps of dirt and gravel. We were on a back road somewhere, with nothing in front of us but brush and darkness and more unpaved road. Bethany had dropped my hand (or I'd dropped hers) and when I held it again, she squeezed back and let it drop again. I tapped her hand a couple of times with my palm, to try and let her know that everything was all right. In a few minutes we came out of the darkness and slowed in front of a brightly lit hotel. We were led out of the car and when my feet hit the cobblestones I realized that I was still wearing my flip -flops. I glanced down and saw that someone had put Bethany's flip -flops back on her feet. I grabbed her hand again as we were led through the empty lobby and up some stairs. They put me into a room and left me there and took the hooded, blue-toed Bethany off somewhere.

The television and phone had been taken out of the room. There was nothing but a bed and a chair. I sat in the chair and waited, and in a few minutes there was a quiet knock on the door and someone entered. It was my uncle.

"I have to be in her room," I said before he could say anything.

"Okay, but . . ."

"You have to put me in with Bethany right now," I said. "Right now."

"Okay, but . . ."

"No, Al. Right now. Come on. Take me in there. Now."

"Okay," he said, finally without the "but," and he took me by the arm and we went to the room next door. Bethany was sitting on the bed, her hood still on and her hands still zip-tied in front of her. Her room was the same as mine, except there was plywood over the window that looked out into the courtyard in the back of the hotel. Al went over and took off her hood and Bethany looked at him and then looked at me.

"You're going home tomorrow," Al said. "Everything's arranged." He cut the plastic zip ties.

"What happened?" I said.

"I don't know," he said. "All I know is you're staying the night and then they'll fly you back tomorrow. I'll have them send some food up in a minute. You're safe. You're both safe. There's nothing to worry about. Everything's arranged and you'll be back home tomorrow."

"Can I call my dad?" I said.

"I'll see if I can get you a phone. You'll get yours tomorrow. But your fathers know. They know you're coming home."

"He paid," Bethany said. She sounded both surprised and disappointed.

"All I know is that you're going home," Al said and left the room.

I didn't know whether to tell Bethany that Al was my uncle or not. I had tried to work it out a couple of different ways in my head, and now I wasn't sure which way to go with it. She didn't know who he was, but why should she? Bethany didn't live in town, and she probably had never been in a hardware store in her life. She was from a family that sent someone to the store. She lived a privileged life, one that would never intersect with my uncle. I decided not to say anything. I might have told her if I thought we'd be friends afterward, or even if we might see each other. She made it clear that I was only there to help her, and only for the duration. I was useful to her only in the short term. I sat and looked at her and was glad I wasn't going to tell her about my uncle.

"That's the way it works," I said. "They pay."

Bethany began to cry. Maybe it was relief, maybe it was the drugs still lingering and messing with her mood, maybe it was exhaustion, or anger. She wanted retribution. Maybe she wanted her dad to come storming through the door like Liam Neeson in *Taken*, maybe she wanted him to give the same speech: "I will look for you, I will find you, and I will kill you." Maybe she wanted a Hollywood rescue. Instead, it was all over with, probably settled before we even got to the hotel, an anticlimax that was going to be nothing more than two very long trips in a private jet that we couldn't even enjoy. I stood and watched her cry and looked down at her freshly polished toes and could only think of *The Big Lebowski*. "I'll get you a toe by this afternoon—with nail polish."

Al came back with a cartful of food and a bottle of wine.

"Take whatever you want," he said. "And if you want something that isn't here, I'll see if I can get it."

"A phone," Bethany said.

"I'm working on it."

"How about I use yours?" Bethany said.

Al raised his hands in resignation. "If I had one. They don't let me bring anything in here that's not approved. I'll wait outside for a bit. Just knock if you need something."

We watched him leave the room: the door opened and we could see two armed men standing there. It looked like Al walked past them and didn't stop, but it was hard to tell in the seconds the door was ajar.

Bethany picked through the food, almost touching all the plates as she sifted through them with her fork. I opened the wine and poured her a full glass.

"What do you suppose happened?" Bethany said. "My father wouldn't pay. Not this fast. Something isn't right."

"You know what I think? I think they fucked up."

"What do you mean?"

"I think they didn't realize who your father was, or who he works for. Something like that. They made the wrong play and that's why we're going home. They fucked up."

"I don't know," she said and paraded her fork around the plates again.

"What do you think happened to Kelly?" she said.

"I hope nothing. I hope they just left her there in the parking lot."

"Why would they?"

"Why wouldn't they? She doesn't have any value to them. Does she?"

"I don't think so."

"Her father doesn't work with yours?"

"No. She doesn't have any money. You don't think she set this up, do you?"

"Why would she do that?"

"Why does anyone do anything? For money."

"You think Kelly's working with a kidnapping outfit in Mexico or Central America or wherever we are?"

"I suppose not. But why would they let her go? She's a witness, right?"

"What could she tell anybody? What did she see? Put yourself in her place. What could you say? Some masked guys got out of a van and grabbed two girls and drove off? Even if they could trace the van, we were probably long gone. What she saw doesn't really matter. And why would they take her? If she doesn't have any money like you say, why would they take her? She'd be more trouble to bring along than to let go."

"But how did they know us. How did they know we'd be together?"

"They've probably been watching us for a while. Maybe they were only going to grab one of us, or both of us separately, and they got lucky. I don't know. Or maybe Kelly was behind it. I don't know her all that well. Do you?"

"I thought I did."

"This is bigger than her," I said. "They killed a couple of guys, you know."

"Who did? What guys?"

"These guys, I'm assuming. Gang guys, cartel guys. I don't know. But the owner of the bar where my dad works was found dead, and the same day another guy was found dead in another bar. You don't know that?"

"No," she said. She stopped eating. She was thinking. I kept talking, feeding her more information, a swirl of what I knew and what I thought I knew.

"You see how it all could be connected. They made a play.

And something happened, something that put an end to it, and we're going to go home."

"You believe them? I don't. Not until they give me a phone. I want to hear it from my dad."

"I don't believe them, but I think we're going home," I said.

"We'll see," Bethany said. "Besides, it won't change anything."

"They'll be home tomorrow," I told [redacted].

"How much is it costing us?" he said.

"They fucked up. It was a mistake."

"A mistake? What does that mean?"

"They were only supposed to rob the warehouse, I guess. Some others took it upon themselves to do the kidnapping. I guess they were following your car and saw your daughter meet mine at the nail salon. They verified who the girls were and sat and waited and when they came out, they grabbed them. They weren't supposed to do any of it. So we don't have to pay anything for their return."

"You believe it?"

"I'm withholding judgment," I said. "We'll see about it when the girls get back. I suspect there's a bigger play here, but I don't know what it is."

"What does Al think?"

"He just wants to get them home," I said. "It could have gone a different way, if he hadn't been involved."

"I suppose. We've never had trouble like this, not like this."

"That's on Fitz and Bishop," I said. "They brought this on. They left us a mess, haven't they?"

"Someone has," he said. "You know what's happening tomorrow?"

"We'll get details when they leave," I said. "I suspect they'll fly them to some small airport and let us know last minute, keep us in the dark as long as possible."

"Any chance we can get the tail number?"

"I'm working on it."

"Al in any danger?"

"I don't think so, but he wouldn't tell me if he was. He has your daughter's best interests in mind, and Sara's. He'll put himself at risk before them. But I don't think we have to worry about it. If Al says they're coming home, then they're coming home."

"So you don't think we have to worry?"

"I don't think we do," I said.

"You worried?"

"Completely."

"We're of the same mind, then."

We landed on a private airfield near Great Barrington. It had been owned by Ryan Salame, former CEO of FTX; it's rumored to be owned by the Saudis now. We didn't care; we wanted to get off the plane as soon as possible and get home.

We'd been the only passengers on the same private jet we'd been forced onto before. They drove us to the airport and handed us our useless phones—the batteries had been drained, and we had no way of charging them until we landed—and two duffel bags stuffed with cash, American dollars. We were to give them to Bethany's dad. We took our seats and watched Mexico City shrink underneath us. It was just me and Bethany. We never saw the pilot or copilot; they stayed behind the locked cabin doors. Al was going to take care of the rest. He stayed in Mexico. I tried to get him to come with us, tried to get him to come home, but he wouldn't. "Don't make me fly all the way back home with her by myself," I said, but even that wouldn't convince him.

Instead, I was alone with Bethany for the duration. She got up from the leather seat over and over and would unzip the duffel bags and look at the money, as if trying to figure out how much she could steal for herself. She would put her hands in among the bundles and move them around, thousands and thousands of dollars literally slipping through her fingers.

"It doesn't make sense," she said. "The money, this bullshit turnaround flight. It doesn't make sense."

"They fucked up," I said.

"You think?" There was a "no duh" quality in that. "Maybe you were wrong about it, wrong about everything. Maybe my father didn't have to pay anything at all."

"Maybe."

She zipped up the duffel and came and sat down across from me.

"What are we going to do about Kelly?" she said.

"I'm not doing anything."

"We need to make her pay. Give her a taste of this."

"A taste of what, this private jet?"

Beth glared at me. "You weren't scared, scared for your life? I know you were. When we were hooded in the back seat, even when we were on the plane, you were squeezing the shit out of my hand."

That was a lie.

"I was scared," I said. "I kept telling myself they weren't going to hurt us. But I was scared."

"We should do that to Kelly," Beth said. "Scare the shit out of her."

"I'm not okay with that. Let's just get home and forget about it."

"I'm not forgetting," she said. "I'm going to get something. How much do you think is in those bags?"

"I don't know," I said. "You could count it."

"We could take some. Just a little. Who would notice?"

"Everyone," I said. "Everyone would notice. I bet they know what's in there down to the dollar."

"You give them way too much credit," she said. "They're not that smart."

"Maybe. But if something goes missing, I don't want it coming back on me."

I could see her stealing something and then blaming me for it. I could totally see it. She scowled at the idea of it and went silent for a while. Not long enough, but for a while at least.

"Maybe we could pay the pilot to take us somewhere," she said. "Somewhere fun. We deserve it."

"Where would you want to go?"

"I don't know. Anywhere. Vegas, LA, Berlin. I don't know. Anywhere."

"I want to go home. Besides, I don't think these planes can go that far."

"You'd be surprised," she said. "I bet they could take us to Las Vegas."

"You should ask them."

Bethany didn't move from her chair.

"You want to go home," she said.

"You don't?"

"Sure, but this is our chance to do something. We've got a private jet and a bunch of cash. Shouldn't we take advantage of it?"

"Honestly," I said. "I want to get off of here as soon as humanly possible."

The plane touched down at night and finally someone emerged from the cabin and without a word opened the door and lowered the steps, and we stepped off onto the grass runway and walked away from the plane. We watched the small jet turn around and take off, and Bethany and I and two duffel bags full of cash waited. There was nothing except the grass runway and a road leading into the darkness.

"What should we do now?" Bethany said.

"We wait. Unless you want to start walking."

She sat down on the duffel bag and looked around. There were the usual stars and a waning moon and a quiet that reached down from somewhere behind the stars and surrounded us with an uneasiness that reminds you how small and insignificant you are. Luckily, we were reminded only for about fifteen minutes before we saw headlights approaching. It was my father. They had contacted him on the descent; he didn't know where we were going to land until then. If my dad was surprised that Al wasn't with us, he didn't betray it to Bethany. He hugged me and hugged her and then asked about the bags. I was going to explain it, but Bethany jumped in and said, "Those are for my father." My father opened the trunk and put the duffels inside, and Bethany and I got into the car and waited for her dad. We waited a good half hour. I wanted him to come so I could get rid of Bethany and get home.

Bethany's father pulled next to us and Bethany rushed out without saying anything to my father or me. My father got out and opened the trunk.

"What's this?" Beth's father said.

"Everything they took. Same amount, clean bills."

"That was fast."

"That was the point, I guess."

"Let's go," Bethany yelled out the window.

"This isn't over," her father said.

"Not by a long shot," my dad said and came back to the car.

He waited for the other car to pull out and then followed.

"I wish you would have brought Zeno," I said.

"I didn't think your friend would like it."

"She's not my friend," I said.

"Al said she was all right."

"He didn't have to be around her the whole time. He didn't have to be alone on a plane with her. When is he coming back, anyway?"

"I was hoping he'd come back with you."

"I tried to get him to. He wouldn't."

"I'll talk to him," he said. "I need him here. We've still got work to do."

I had to go to school the next morning. I didn't want to go, but my dad insisted. At least I'd have an interesting story to tell.

I really only went to see Kelly. She was standing outside the front doors, waiting for me as I walked up. She was as cool as ever, if not more, wearing vintage Boston Celtics Chuck Ts, wide-legged black pants with ragged cuffs that fell exactly above childlike flower-print white socks and a waist that rode low on the right side, exposing an enticing triangle of hip that would have the whole building weak, a bulky blue sweater over a mustard T-shirt, and a green trucker cap that perfectly matched her shoes. The trucker cap had the image of dog on it, just the head in profile, mouth open, teeth exposed, with "Beware" printed above it.

"Thanks for dressing up for me," I teased.

She shrugged it off with a laugh and a hug and said, "From the cartel to the classroom, it's just one hostage situation to another. Haven't you suffered enough?"

"It never ends."

"We've got to get you out of here," Kelly said. "You need to taste some freedom."

I almost agreed. "I need to go to class," I said.

It didn't last. Kelly was bugging me in between every bell.

"I need to hear about everything," she texted me during class. "Now." School was somewhere else, the teachers a grinding hum off in the distance. I was still off in a hotel in Mexico or in a plane with bags of cash at my feet, or off somewhere else telling Kelly all about it. I lasted until lunch and then Kelly and I ditched. She drove and I talked. I told her as much as I could remember.

"You didn't tell me about Bethany," she said. "How horrible was she?"

"She was fine."

"No, she wasn't."

"She was. She was fine."

"I hate to hear it," she said. "I'm not going to believe it."

"You don't have to," I said. I don't know why I lied to her. Maybe I didn't feel like beating up on Bethany after what we'd been through.

Kelly took off her cap and pulled it down on my head, laughing as she pulled it lower and lower.

"She was fine because of you," she said. "That's why. I should have been there. I wish I had been there."

I lifted the cap over my eyes. "It was better this way. My dad's not going to forget what you did."

"What did I do? Got his daughter kidnapped. That's all I did."

"Well, he appreciates it," I said and put the cap back on her head.

"You suppose Bethany hates me?"

"You suppose I believe that you care?"

"We should all go get our nails done again," Kelly said.

"You like trouble," I said.

She shrugged, and we drove around some more until it was

time for school to be done. We drove out past the golf course, and out past the Living Faith Church, and out past the cemetery and on out of town. We drove until we hit the propane tanks across from the ball field and then looped back, past the Dollar Tree and the Dunkin' and the state forest, and then back into town. Kelly looked at the time.

"We could have actually gone somewhere," she said.

"Like where?"

"I don't know. Someplace new. Some place that isn't this. We could be in Boston or New York in the time we took driving around."

"Next time."

"Next time. Where to now?"

"You want to go by the hardware store?" I said. "My dad wants to talk to you."

"About what?"

"I don't know. Maybe he wants to talk to you about the books you gave him. Maybe he wants to offer you a job."

I was kidding, but I'd said the wrong thing. She was closing off, retreating the way I'd seen her do with lots of other people, but usually not me. Her eyes were hard and mean. She was like Al that way, angry and distant and wanting to be alone.

"I'll take you back to your car," she said. I figured she'd drop me off and then head off on her own.

"No," I said. "Let's go together. He just wants to talk. Show some appreciation, you know? He's grateful, that's all. We'll go together. You'll see. Maybe he'll take us to dinner. Maybe he'll take you someplace new. Like Mexico."

"With a bag over my head," she said.

"With your best friend Bethany. Come on, let's go see him."

"I should have been with you," she said.

"It's over with."

"I was worried. Fuck if I wasn't worried."

"It worked out fine. That's what my dad wants to tell you. Everything's fine. Let's go see him."

"Is your uncle going to be there?"

"There's nothing to worry about there, believe me. And no, he won't be there. It'll just be the three of us. As quick as you want it to be. I want you to meet him. You're going to be part of this, whether you want to or not."

"It is a hostage situation, then."

"You don't want to meet my dad?"

"Maybe not today. Give him some time, you know."

"You'll have to sooner or later. Might as well be sooner, when he's got gratitude, you know?"

She thought about it. She glanced at herself in the rearview and then looked over to me. Her eyes were soft again, playful. She was back; the retreat had been reversed.

"Should I keep the cap on?"

"He's going to love it," I said.

Dale Avery was looking at mousetraps. He was examining snap traps and glue strips and electronic traps that send an alert to your phone when they've killed a mouse. He wasn't going to buy any of them, but he was giving them all ample consideration. I wasn't going to say anything to him; I was only walking by when he said (without looking up), "Which of these would you use?"

"Snap," I said. Dale was startled by my voice. He was expecting someone else.

"Al around?"

"Not today," I said.

"He still alive?" Dale said.

"He is."

"You wouldn't know it by coming here."

"You want a cup of coffee?" I said, and Dale and I walked over to the market across the street. This was what Al did. This was why people liked him and why people like Dale missed him when he was gone. I bought Dale a cup of coffee and we went and sat at a couple of the six chairs they had at the market and I didn't know what to say. Dale didn't know what to say either, so we sat and drank our coffee and looked out the window over at the hardware store as if we were both looking for the same person to arrive.

"He didn't drop dead, did he?" Dale said.

"He's fine, Dale. He'll be back in a day or two."

"You found Fitz is what I heard."

"I did."

"And Al found Bishop."

"I don't think that's true," I said.

"That's what I heard."

"Who told you that?"

"One of the EMT guys."

"Which EMT? Our EMTs weren't on the scene."

"They talk. Or heard it on the radio. I don't know. I only know what they tell me."

"Al was with me, Dale."

"Not when the EMTs came."

"No. I sent him home. He didn't need to be around that. It triggered him, you know, with Vera and everything. But he was with me. What difference does it make, anyway?"

"It doesn't make any difference to me. I just thought it was an amazing coincidence that you found one dead guy and Al found another."

"It would be amazing. It would be astronomical, almost impossible. Except it didn't happen. It's amazing enough that they both died the same day. But I bet a lot of people had heart attacks that day. Someone's trying to make it more amazing than it really was."

"Two thousand."

"Excuse me?"

"Two thousand people die every day from heart attacks. In the US," Dale said. "I looked it up."

"There you go. That's a lot."

"You ever had a heart attack?"

"No. You?"

"Two. Neither was in a bar, though."

"Where were you?"

"The first one I was home. EMTs saved my life. The second I was in the doctor's office. Flopped right there on the floor."

"It happens, I guess."

"I live my life," Dale said. "I have my coffee with Al in the morning and go about my business, thankful for what I've got."

"I understand."

"I sure would miss Al if he wasn't around," he said. "But he doesn't need to know that."

Dale Avery finished his coffee and got up from his chair and left without a word and walked across the road to his car and drove off. I sat and wondered if he was trying to tell me something.

I went back to the hardware store and got Zeno, who was asleep behind the counter, and drove over to the bar, wondering if I should tell Al about my conversation with Avery. I decided against it. There were a few people working in the kitchen when I arrived. We were getting ready to reopen. Fitz's will had put the place back on me; I could buy it at the current assessment, with the money going to a few charities Fitz had listed, along with duly noted amounts for each charity. It was an agreement we'd settled on when he bought the place and he must have forgotten to change it. He wouldn't have agreed to it if he'd known how things were going to play out. That's the trouble with planning for a future; the one you figured on never comes.

I went into the kitchen and made a nuisance of myself and everyone ignored me and doted on Zeno, giving him slices of zucchini and steak and chicken parts, which he would have happily eaten all day long. I took Zeno and we went and sat at a table near the bar. Zeno stretched out on the floor, settling in for a long nap with a treat-filled belly. I watched his eyes grow heavy and I doomscrolled through depressing news of the world and no word from anyone I cared about. I was killing time before I got summoned to meet with the boss. I was surprised that he hadn't called me already. Maybe he was spending time with Bethany. Maybe he was counting his money. I wasn't going to call him. I knew I wouldn't have to.

It didn't take long.

"I'll be there," I said.

"And how about Al?"

"Not yet," I said. "He had a couple of loose ends he wanted to tend to, he said."

I went back to the kitchen and told them that I was leaving. No one cared. I just owned the place. Zeno and I went out to my car and there was Al, parked next to me.

"Why didn't you tell me you were back?"

"I literally just got here," he said.

"And we've got to go," I said. "Come on. I'll drive."

He'd taken a commercial flight back, the last one out, leaving just before midnight. He didn't look tired. He looked good. I was glad to see him. We drove and I told him to sleep if he wanted. He didn't need it, he said.

"I had coffee with Dale Avery this morning," I told him. "He asked about you."

"He's probably been worried. He likes his routine."

"He got me worried. Said he heard from some EMT guy that you were at Bishop's Corner."

"No one listens to what Dale says. He talks like he knows something, but he doesn't. He always has his wires crossed."

"An electrician joke?"

"I didn't mean it," Al said. "I swear I didn't mean it. Maybe I'm not ready to be back."

"Are you, though?"

He shrugged. "I think so. For now, anyway. I can still build my house down there."

"You've got time to figure it out."

"I should go down there more," he said. "See if I actually like it."

"Your father could send his jet for you."

"If he had a jet."

"He can have one soon enough," I said.

"After he pays me back. After that he can do whatever he wants."

"His got big plans."

"So he says."

"Well, he talks a good game," I said.

"That he does," Al said.

I had my eyes on the road but hardly noticed the familiar fields, the usual houses and landmarks, as they passed in a steady rhythm while we drove toward the city. I was in my head, formulating something I wanted to tell Al. I wanted to get it out in the open, the anger and distrust he had in me at the start of all of this, how he thought the wrong things, and how I had too. Maybe not for the first time, but for the longest time, we'd been on opposite sides of an issue, ready to fight, ready to go to war with each other when we never should have. I was working on what to say and how to say it, how to tell him how we were lucky to have gotten past it, how we were back on the same side the way we always should be, but only through luck or circumstance, not through communication and cooperation. I wanted to tell him that we need to talk more, to be truly open and honest with each other at all times, so we can stop any animosity before it ever begins. I was working on the right way to say it (better than I'm saying it here), but once I was ready to say something, I looked over and saw Al sleeping in the passenger seat, his head tipped back, his mouth slack and slightly open. He slept all the way, even until after I'd pulled into the parking garage, even after I'd parked the car and turned off the engine. I put my hand on his shoulder and he snapped awake.

"You ready?" I said.

"I can be."

"He doesn't know you're here, but you're the one he wants to talk to."

"Okay."

"Okay?"

"Yeah. Let's go."

We didn't talk as we walked into the building; we didn't talk as we rode the elevator; and we didn't talk as we waited outside the office. I let Al figure it out. He didn't need my help.

"This is a surprise," said when he saw Al.

"Everything get back to you all right?" Al said.

"Down to the dollar."

"And Beth?"

"Bethany. She'll be all right. I'm not sure I can say the same thing about me."

"I have something else for you," Al said. "Something to show you." He brought out his phone and held it toward so he could see. "This is the man who was responsible for taking the girls. Or so they tell me."

It was a dimly lit video of a corpse, a dead man lying on a concrete floor in blood-stained clothes. The camera moved over the body, showing the wounds, the bloody clothes, the motionless body, the empty eye sockets. It lasted less than forty-five seconds. I didn't know what to make of it. I don't know if the video was real or not. Maybe it had been CGI or AI generated (one of the hands appeared to have more than the usual number of fingers, but it was hard to tell) or they had used an old video from somewhere else, or they had supplied the body themselves. I suppose it didn't matter. I didn't care. The video wasn't for me; it didn't have to convince me. It only had to put an idea in one person's mind. I stopped watching it after a few seconds and tried to watch ██████ to get a read on his reaction. He was expressionless, studying the video as if maybe he'd recognize the man in it. Whether he believed the body was the person responsible for kidnapping his daughter, I don't know, but he believes in the violence, the ability to commit it, and the message of it.

"What do you think?" ██████ asked.

"It was a mistake, they tell me," Al said.

"You believe that?"

I was about to say something stupid and counterproductive, when Al thankfully cut me off.

"When Caesar wanted to conquer the Gauls," he said, "he built a bridge across the Rhine. No one had ever done this before. It was an unbelievable feat, beyond the Gauls' imagination—like someone landing a spaceship in your driveway—but Caesar built it, marched his troops across it and then turned around and marched back across. Then he burned it into the river. Destroyed the bridge, this amazing, unimaginable creation. He'd made his point. He could do it again. He could do it whenever he wanted. That was the whole point of it, and I think that's what this was. They took your money, they took the girls, then they gave them right back. They made their point. Now they want to deal."

"So what should we do?"

"We don't take the deal they offered, but close to it. And we give them some benchmarks. They moved some money for you once, a lot of money, on a quick turnaround. More than Peck and I can move, and faster. But can they do it consistently? And can they do more than convert it to clean cash? We should figure out how much you want them to move and how often and where, and hold them to it. They're not partners, they're subs. Make them work for their money, just like everybody else."

"You can put that together, right, Peck?"

I nodded. "I just need some information and then I can get it to you tomorrow. I should say, though, if they can keep this up, you're not going to need Al and me anymore," I said.

shook his head. "I'm going to need you to watch over things."

"I'll watch the bar, like always. And Al can go back to the hardware store. But on salary. We don't need a cut. You're going to have too many hands in here."

"We'll see," he said. "And I'm supposed to forget about what they did to Bethany?"

"You don't forget," Al said, "but you wait. We make it part of the negotiation, but we don't forget. We keep it close for a while, and wait for the right time. If they took care of the right guy we'll find another way, but if the guy really responsible is still around, I'll take care of him personally. I'm an honest broker, as far as they're concerned. Let them continue to think it."

"You played it like Peck would have," he said.

"It's the smart play, for now. Isn't it, Peck?"

I agreed. Al had it covered. He was more persuasive than I was, more convincing, and less courteous, I guess.

We went back to the car, where Zeno was sitting in the passenger seat, waiting patiently. Al opened the door and gave Zeno a tight hug and rubbed him under his chin and gently on the top of his snout. Zeno closed his eyes in enjoyment.

"I didn't even know you were there," Al said to Zeno.

"You're awake now. So is he."

Al scratched Zeno behind the ear and motioned to the back seat and Zeno made way for him in the front. Zeno stretched out on his blanket in the back and was asleep again by the time we were back on the road.

"You still have your hard drive?" I asked Al.

"Why wouldn't I?'

"I don't know. Because you said it didn't have anything on it."

"It's got two million dollars on it."

"And how far will that get you?"

"As far as the next two million, and the next after that."

"I want that hard drive," I said. "But not the two million. You understand?"

"I think so."

"We've got to get you set, Al."

"I appreciate that. I really do."

"It's all right."

We drove straight to Al's and went into his office in the garage. He transferred his crypto off the small, black hard drive and into an online wallet. It wasn't going to stay there. He'd transfer it to a different drive as soon as he got one and put it in his safe. I needed the original drive, and I needed what he'd left on it, a bunch of encrypted files, eleven, to be exact, amounting to about seventy-three gigabytes of data. It was what I had feared. Al could have compiled a lot of information over the years, just loading shell after shell into the chamber until he was ready to fire. I wondered how it all would have gone if Sara hadn't taken the goddam thing in the first place. He'd told me straight to my face that there was nothing on it, and here I was looking at it. Maybe he wouldn't have gone through with it. It wasn't worth thinking about; Al had given it to me now. I could do whatever I wanted with the files. I opened one named SourceIP_hext.txt. It looked like random alphanumeric characters.

Another encoded document. I didn't know what to do with it, so I closed out and opened another file, but was again faced with gibberish, rows of random numbers or non-English letters and symbols.

"What is this stuff?" I said.

"It's either the stuff that can put us all in jail or junk I pulled off the internet, random shit you could never decode. Maybe both. Do you want to know?"

"I'd rather not," I said and drove Al back to the bar so he could get his car. I parked and he got out and I got out too. "You want to come in?" I said. "Raise a glass to our good fortune?"

"Maybe later. I'll come by to see Sara after she gets home."

"I'll text you."

Al drove off. Zeno moved back into the passenger seat. He didn't want to go inside. He wanted to go home. So we drove home. I put the hard drive in the glove compartment and waited for Sara to get home from school. She was late.

She looked into her coffee, staring into the over-creamed surface, and then said what she'd wanted to say all along.

"I think I deserve something for my effort," my mother said.

"What effort was that?"

"I tipped you off. Otherwise, your father would be in jail right now. Instead, he's living the life he's wanted all along."

That wasn't true. She knew it wasn't true. I pushed my empty cup away from me and leaned back in the booth.

"Al wasn't going to do anything. He never was."

She shrugged. "You don't know. I was told something and passed it along, to help your father and to help you. Al was ready, that's what I was told. And now everyone's safe. I'm not asking for anything, but you'd think I'd have a little gratitude, a little something for my part."

"I'd think that helping to keep us safe would be enough. Keeping me safe. And Dad, and Al. Isn't that worth something?"

"It is," she said. "That's worth everything. But I need to be safe too. I put myself at risk. A lot of risk. I don't expect your father to care about that, or even know about it, but I think I should get something, not much, just something, for my help.

He's got enough, doesn't he? And that's partly because of me. I helped out when he needed it. I could use a little help, just a little. That's all I'm saying."

"You helped yourself enough," I said. "You took what you wanted. You got the life you wanted, didn't you?"

I could see the tears fill her eyes. She tried to not wipe them away, to fight them back, but there they were, large pools of water waiting to drop down her cheeks.

"I'm on my own," she said.

I wasn't sad for her. There weren't going to be any tears in my eyes. I looked at her and realized I didn't care one way or the other. That was her life. I wished I could care for her; I wished she'd been around for all the tears that I'd cried when she left, all the tears my father cried. She should have seen us then. I wanted a mother; I desperately wanted my mother then. Now, now was too late. I didn't feel sorry; I didn't feel sympathy; I didn't feel anything. I couldn't even fake it.

"If I ask him," I said, "I'm sure Dad would give you something. You want me to ask?"

The tears were gone. She was composed again, hard and stern. "I think it's right that I get something. I still know things."

"That's how you want this to go? You're not asking now?"

"However you want to play it," she said.

"I want to be clear about this," I said. "You're not asking. You still know things. That's your position on this."

"I don't want much," she said. "I want your father to be safe. I can do that for him. It won't take much."

"Ok," I said. "Everything's a fucking transaction with you."

"With everybody," she said. "It's that way with everybody."

I looked at the empty cup on the table. I looked at her cup, full of cold, tan coffee. This wasn't going to happen again, I realized. My mother was right, she was on her own.

"You ever been bitten by a dog?" I asked her.

I drove into the city and parked in the garage and took a briefcase of money with me. It was lighter than usual, a lot lighter. The rest of it was delivered by people Al's father had hired. We didn't know them, we didn't see them, but they would arrive three times a week, cleaning about four times the amount Al and I had ever done on our best week. Al's father was taking nine percent, five for himself, and Al and I split the other four. And he was paying back some of the money Al had put into the hotel, a percentage was coming out of the bookings, Saudis and Chinese and Americans who paid for rooms they never used, some of them paying multiples on the rates. A Russian general offered Al ten times the value for his empty lot. Al didn't sell.

"Maybe I'll still build," he said.

"You should build now," I told him. "Get it ready."

"I don't want it to be ready before I am," he said.

He had the hardware store again, and I owned the bar. Bishop's was sold off and bled dry in a matter of months. It didn't matter.

But that was all in the future. I put a leash on Zeno and grabbed the briefcase with my other hand and walked into the building. I was stopped by security. The guy knew me, had seen me plenty of times, but never with Zeno. It threw him for a second, made him more cop-like than usual.

"I'm sorry, but you can't take a dog in here, Peck."

"I'll only be a minute," I said. "I just want to show him to somebody in the office, for adoption. I'm just going up and I'll be right back down."

He looked at Zeno and then back at me. Maybe he knew why I was there; I didn't know. He wouldn't see me again. "That's a big dog," he said. "You couldn't bring a little Yorkie or something?"

"This is the dog they wanted to see," I told him. "Rescue. Was just surrendered by his owner. I'll make it quick."

"They can't come down?" he said.

I shrugged. "You know how that goes. I just do what I'm told, and I was told to bring him up. We could call up and ask. You want to ask him?"

He looked at Zeno again and then said, "Follow me." He led us to a spot to the side of the elevators, a secluded spot off the lobby where no one could see us. He called for the elevator and when it came, he checked to make sure it was empty and motioned for us to get on. "Take an empty on your way back down," he said. "I could get in trouble for this, you know."

"You and me both," I said. "I won't be long."

Zeno sat and watched the numbers of the floors light up. We walked into the office and [redacted] gave Zeno an annoyed glance and was maybe going to say something, but I got right to it. I took the hard drive out of my jacket pocket and put it on the desk.

"I don't think he'd ever do anything with it," I said. "But I got it for you anyway."

"Do I want to know what's on it?"

"Nothing good," I said. "Spreadsheets and photographs and phone messages. There might even be messages from you to Fitz, giving him the go -ahead to come after Al and me."

"That wasn't the play, Peck."

"I don't believe you." I looked over at Zeno, sitting perfectly still, leaning forward a little, his dark eyes fixed on ██████, waiting. "And don't waste my time trying to explain. I know what you told him."

"Does Al know?"

"If Al knew you'd be in a ditch somewhere, or on a video getting handed around, as proof of what happens to people like you. So I know and you know. And that's enough for now. You shouldn't have let it play like that. You should have come to me. After all these years, you should have talked to me. I could have made it work, any way you wanted. Instead, you let that idiot Fitz tell you what to do."

"They said you were turning evidence. And here you are with this." He waved his hand at the small black device on his desk and Zeno followed his hand, his large head leaning forward. I tugged on his leash and he settled back down, still alert, his eyes fixed on the man in front of him.

"Is this evidence? Maybe it is. Or maybe it's garbage, just a bunch of files, encoded and encrypted, designed to make it look like something it's not, designed to confuse and deflect. I know what I'm doing. You should know that. And if you had any doubts, you could have asked me. You could have asked me what's on there, and I would have told you then. I would have told you exactly what's on there. But not now. You had to go and listen to Fitz, put your trust in him and Bishop. And how'd that work out? So now I'm not going to tell you. You'll have to figure it out, and you'll have to wonder if it's the only copy. That's where we are. I would have handed this over; I would have walked away, let Fitz take over, if that's what you wanted. But you see how your way went. They got you mixed up with people who know what they're doing. Fitz did that. He brought this trouble on you, and Al and I got the best deal for you that we could. Could Fitz have done that? Can you imagine it? Still, you're better off, aren't you? Because of Al and me."

I took the money out of the case and put it on the desk next to the drive. Zeno watched with his German shepherd face, steady and intent.

"This is the last time we'll see each other, and you won't see Al again either. We're finished, and that's it."

He picked up the drive and held it uncomfortably in his palm. "What should I do with it?"

"I'd take it and grind it into dust and bury it at the bottom of the ocean and forget about it."

"You have copies."

"I won't tell you." I said. "But I will tell you that the DA doesn't have it, and Al doesn't have it. As far as I know, there's not a copy of it anywhere else. And I'm telling you this directly; if anyone has a copy, it's me. And if I do, it's someplace safe, with instructions for the DA or whoever on how to open the documents. Maybe it exists. Maybe it doesn't. I've always been straight with you, but you took that off the table. You did that. So, I'll leave you with a question. Would you trust me with it if I did have it?"

"Yes."

"Okay, then," I said, and Zeno and I left.

I didn't believe him. Maybe he'd let it go. He was making more money than he'd ever made, and if he can keep the doubt out of his mind, he'll have nothing to worry about. I don't think he can. I'm hoping he proves me wrong, but if he has to find out, he'll be making a mistake. If he wants a war, I'll give him a war. If he wants to play games, I'll play. I know how to play this.

GRATITUDES

I wrote this novel in the months after the death of my father. And the writing of it was a surprise. In the immediate weeks after, I wasn't sure that I could write anything; I wasn't sure that I wanted to write at all anymore. And for a while, I didn't. For the first time in a long, long time, I didn't write anything one day, and then I didn't the next, and as the days piled up I worried that I wouldn't be able to get back to it ever again.

Everything always starts small, a phrase (*As Simple As Snow*) or a fragment of conversation (*Just Thieves*), something that captures my attention and won't let go. It's like finding a really good nail and realizing you have to build a house, without knowing what the house looks like, knowing nothing except the impulse to build it. For me, for *All We Trust*, the nail was "I won't tell you my father was a criminal." I tried to get rid of it – I didn't want to write about my father, anyone's father – but I kept returning to that sentence, trying to figure out who was saying it and why. I wasn't getting very far, and wasn't doing any writing at this point, just stuck on that one sentence, frustrated and worried that I was wasting my time.

I begin every day with a walk with our dog, Ruth. Every day, for more than eight years. First thing in the morning, sometimes even before the sun is up, we're out the door walking along the quiet roads near our house. Ruth finds her stories in the scents and smells she encounters, and I try to organize my thoughts, think about characters or stories, or sentences, paragraphs, or, if I'm lucky, pages that I'll be able to put down when we get back home. Only, I hadn't really been doing that lately. I didn't want to be in my head, didn't want to think about a father and crime and loss and grief. But there was that nail. Then, one morning, Ruth and I were walking up our hill, when we saw black smoke. From our angle, it looked as if a house was on fire, but as we made our way up the hill, we could see that it wasn't, but the image unlocked something. I knew what to do with that nail; I suddenly had a shitload of them, and lumber, and at least a rough idea what the finished thing would look like. And it would be about a father and crime and loss and grief. And *All We Trust* is a product of anger, anxiety, and grief, but it's also a product of gratitude. I'm incredibly grateful to my dad, my family and friends, and people I've never met in person—readers and librarians and teachers and booksellers—who provided comfort, encouragement, and support. I'm lucky to be surrounded with people (many of whom have been around a long, long time) who are smarter and kinder than I am. Thank you all.

I specifically want to mention the following, who were instrumental in helping with *All We Trust*—some of them didn't make it from beginning to end, from writing to publication, and some I relied on (heavy at times), but everyone contributed in significant and meaningful ways – and I greatly benefited from their hard work and generosity: Deb Aaronson, Michael Barson, Carl Bromley, Michelle Capone, Beste Doğan, David Halpern, John Kenyon, Karen Krumpak, Gina Maolucci, [illegible], Janet Oshiro, Kathy Robbins, and everyone at TRO.

About the Author

GREGORY GALLOWAY is the author of *Just Thieves*, *The 39 Deaths of Adam Strand*, and the Alex Award–winning *As Simple As Snow*. His short stories have appeared in the *Burning Down the House*, *Rush Hour*, and *Taking Aim* anthologies. He is a graduate of the Iowa Writers' Workshop and currently resides in Connecticut.